Charles James Fox

Letters of the Ghost of Alfred

Addressed to the Hon. Thomas Erskine

Charles James Fox

Letters of the Ghost of Alfred
Addressed to the Hon. Thomas Erskine

ISBN/EAN: 9783337147228

Printed in Europe, USA, Canada, Australia, Japan

Cover: Foto ©Andreas Hilbeck / pixelio.de

More available books at **www.hansebooks.com**

OF THE

GHOST OF ALFRED,

ADDRESSED TO THE

Hon. THOMAS ERSKINE,

AND THE

Hon. CHARLES JAMES FOX,

ON THE OCCASION OF THE STATE TRIALS AT
THE CLOSE OF THE YEAR 1794, AND THE
BEGINNING OF THE YEAR 1795.

―――――――――

" Fuere tamen cives, qui feque, remque publicam obftinatis
" animis perditum irent.—Tanta vis morbi, atqui uti tabes
" plerofque civium animos invarerat."—*Sall. Bell. Cat.*

―――――――――

London:

PRINTED FOR J. WRIGHT, OPPOSITE OLD BOND-STREET,
PICCADILLY.

1798.

EDITOR's ADVERTISEMENT.

THE following Letters were publi∫hed ∫eparately in the True Briton, on the occa∫ion of the State Trials which took place at the clo∫e of the year 1794, *and at the beginning of the year* 1795. *The topics to which they relate are among the mo∫t important that can occupy the minds of Britons. The Editor feels it a duty which he owes to his Countrymen to recall their attention to the contents of the∫e Letters, which, he is ∫orry to ∫ay, are ∫till as ∫ea∫onable as when they were written. Their objects are, to pre∫erve*

the

the administration of justice in its genuine purity ; to vindicate the principles of English jurisprudence, respecting the crime of High Treason; and to render the laws what they ought ever to be, " a terror to evil-doers, and a praise and pro-" tection to them that do well"—To correct the irregular, indecent, and unconstitutional practices of those advocates, who seem to have taken a general retainer for the domestic, as a correspondent class of senators have for the foreign enemies of the country—To lay open the wiles and artifices of French Revolutionary Treason— To rescue Trial by Jury from the fallacies and false doctrines, by which factious and seditious men seek to render it, not only a shelter for the worst of crimes, but an engine of destruction to the Constitution itself—To expose the sophistry with which a Jacobinical Opposition have insolently contended, and still insolently contend, that because the prisoners tried for High Treason were acquitted, no treasonable conspiracy had existed—And, finally, to exhibit, in just colours, the

2

the unexampled profligacy of the same desperate party, in extolling, patronising, and promoting that horrid and destructive system of Revolution and Anarchy, which has already proved the most dreadful scourge that ever afflicted the human race, and which threatens to lay the whole fabric of civil society in ruins.

That the publication of these Letters may conduce to the maintenance and security of that Constitution, among the founders of which we have ever been proud to reckon the great and venerable character, whose shade here speaks to us with a Warning Voice,

Is the fervent prayer of

May 21, 1798.   *THE EDITOR.*

LETTER I.

To the Hon. *THOMAS ERSKINE.*

SIR,

THE profecutions for High Treafon, which have lately been inftituted by Government, are likely to form an important Epoch in the Hiftory of this Country, and may poffibly involve the fate of the Conftitution itfelf.

The conduct of every individual engaged in fuch momentous proceedings, fhould be fubjected to the niceft fcrutiny, but that of fo diftinguifhed a member as yourfelf of the profeffion to which you belong, muft be expected to excite particular attention. Making every allowance for the zeal of an advocate, I am forry to fay that in fome refpects your conduct during the Trial of HARDY, deferves the fevereft animadverfion. I do not allude merely to the pains you took to divert the minds of the Jury from thofe parts of the evidence, which moft affected the Prifoner, nor upon the dexterity with which you directed their attention to matters that were quite foreign and irrelevant. I do not mean to expofe the many unfair advantages you

B   took

took of the unavoidable prolixity and com-
plication of the cafe, arifing out of the nature
and extent of the Confpiracy, which it was neceffary to unfold—a Confpiracy compofed of fo
many branches, purfued by fo many channels,
and comprizing, if fully ftated, the internal
hiftory of the Country for above two years.—
Neither fhall I animadvert upon your bold un-
dertaking, to convince the Jury that a treafonable Confpiracy had no real exiftence, although
it had been ftrictly inveftigated, and folemnly
affirmed by both Houfes of Parliament; although
it had been found by a Grand Jury, (for other-
wife they would not have put the Prifoner
upon his trial); and although every man in the
kingdom believes, that if the plans and defigns
which were proved to have conftituted that Confpiracy, had been effected, the Government would
have been totally overthrown. Still lefs am I difpofed to arraign you for endeavouring, as you
were undoubtedly intitled to do, to perfuade the
Jury that the Prifoner was not implicated in this
Confpiracy (even if it had exifted); although, in
his character as Secretary, he was neceffarily privy
to the whole of the plot, and although he fuper-
added the zeal of a Leader to the activity of an
induftrious Agent. Thefe confiderations all related
to matters, in which the effect of fuch artifices and
mifreprefentations might be obviated by the good
                                            fenfe

fenfe of the Jury, aided by the obfervations of the Counfel for the profecution, and by the authentic ftatements of the Judge.

My object in now addreffing you, is to point out your grofs infringement on the eftablifhed practice of the Courts upon Trials by Jury, and your equally grofs violation of the fundamental principles of the judicial part of the Conftitution, by taking upon yourfelf to lay down the law to the Jury. There is no principle of the Conftitution better eftablifhed or more important than *that* which preferves the important diftinction of law and fact, by referring *the Law to the Court, and the Fact to the Jury.* This is the grand fafeguard and barrier of the laws of the Realm, and the only fecurity for their due adminiftration. But to have heard you for hours addreffing the Jury on the Law, arguing points, quoting cafes, and ranfacking authorities, one would have thought either that there was no Judge on the Bench, or that you fancied yourfelf to be there. The abfurdity of fuch conduct is equal to its irregularity. The Judge is placed by the Conftitution on the Bench, not as a cypher, nor merely to preferve the forms of proceeding, and to fum up the evidence, but to inftruct and direct the Jury, as far as is neceffary, in matters of Law. It is from him, and from

him alone, that the Jury are to derive their information of the Law, as far as the Law applies to
the cafe. Entitled to give a general verdict, both
of Law and Fact, and not being qualified by
their education and habits of life to decide upon
queftions of law (for a man may make a moft
excellent Juryman who has never in his whole life
feen a Law book) Juries are to be guided in that
part of their duty which involves the confideration
and decifion of the Law, folely by the light
which they receive from the Bench; and by attending to any other light, they only expofe
themfelves to be misled. Counfel are not entitled to the leaft credit on this fubject. They
cannot, indeed, altogether refrain from fpeaking
on the legal part of the cafe, in bringing the *general* charge home to the Prifoner, or in repelling
that charge; but in fo doing, inftead of going
into elaborate arguments, citing cafes, difcuffing
abftract principles, and groping for nice and hait-
breadth diftinctions, (all which is perfectly regular when they are addreffing the Judges,) they
are bound, as well by the immemorial ufage of
the profeffion, as by the reafon and decency of
the thing, in their addreffes to Juries, to refer
the validity of any obfervations they may for that
purpofe be obliged to make on the Law, to
the opinion and correction of the Judge.

It

It has, therefore, been the conſtant practice, whenever a diſtinct point of Law has occurred, which it became neceſſary to argue, for the Counſel to turn from the Jury, and to addreſs themſelves ſolely to the Bench. And in their obſervations upon the general caſe, whenever they have been obliged to touch upon legal topics, they have been accuſtomed to employ ſuch language as this:—" Gentlemen of the " Jury, his Lordſhip will tell you that this is " Law; on this ſubject I ſpeak entirely under, " his correction; and whatever I ſay on the " legal part of the caſe is entitled to no weight " in your minds, unleſs it be confirmed by " the Bench." This is the only regular, correct and decent ſtyle, in which a Counſel can ſay any thing to a Jury on the ſubject of Law. But you, as if you thought it neceſſary, in favour of *that* cauſe for which you ſeem to have received a general retainer, to violate all eſtabliſhed principles and uſages, and *this* at a time when they ſhould be more ſcrupulouſly adhered to than ever, arrogate to yourſelf a right to which you have not the leaſt title, and thereby encroach on the province of the Judge by laying down the Law to the Jury, It is to no purpoſe that you affect to diſclaim all reſpect and authority as to your own opinion, by re-ferring that opinion to the authorities of H.... .

HOLT, COKE, and MANSFIELD, and other venerable luminaries of the Law. Your opinion, however founded and supported, and however valuable to those who may pay for it, is not, *in the eye of the Law*, worth one farthing, nor are any authorities of the least weight *in your mouth*. It is the opinion of the Judge, who presides at the Trial, and whose authority you cannot mould to your purpose, to which alone you are entitled to refer; it is the living Judge, constitutionally placed on the Bench, and presumed to be master of all the ancient authorities, and of all the learning on the subject, who is, by the aid of his study and experience, and under the obligation of his oath, to give the Jury sound directions on the matter of Law. Further assistance the Constitution supposes not necessary to be afforded a Jury, for it has afforded them no other. While to secure to the accused, not merely a fair and impartial Trial, but also the benefit of every advantage that his case can afford, it has imposed on the Judge the additional duty of acting as Counsel for the Prisoner. A better Counsel he cannot have if really innocent. And while the Judges, being independent of the Crown, are superior to all suspicion of undue influence, their declaration of the Law is delivered in so public and open a manner, that it not only involves their own reputation, but

but may be fubjected to future revifion. On the other hand, the advocate has neither competence, refponfibility, nor impartiality. However able, he has no *conftitutional* competence, for no truft is repofed in him except by the party for whom he appears. He has no refponfibility, except to that party, for whom he engages to do his beft. And he cannot be impartial, for by the nature of his fituation he is engaged on one fide, and, as a noble Judge has obferved, *is bound not to be convinced,* He is a Swifs, and fights for pay—and he perfectly exemplifies the Proverb, " *Point d'Argent, point de Suiffe."*

That the Council for the Dean of St. Afaph, fhould fail in refpect to the Bench, or attempt to ufurp the functions of the Judge, may not, however, excite much furprize. But what fhall be faid of the Barrifter who can fo far difgrace his Robe—that Robe too, honourably diftinguifhed by the favour of the Crown—as to promulgate, in his profeffional character, and in the Tribunals of Juftice, the moft feditious of doctrines? What fhall be faid of the Advocate, who, while pleading for a prifoner charged with the groffeft violation of the duty of a fubject, takes advantage of that freedom of fpeech which is allowed him for very different purpofes, to in-

fult

fult the Majefty of his Sovereign, by declaring that the people have a right to change their Government, and that the Monarch on the Throne, derives his title from the exercife of fuch a right. Such were the doctrines openly avowed by you on the Trial of Hardy, and never before I will venture to affert, was fo grofs, fo audacious a contempt offered to the adminiftration of Juftice.

It would be eafy to prove that this your doctrine is falfe in the *abftract*—that a right in the people to change their Government, is incompatible with the duties of fubjects, and the nature of fociety—that it is repugnant to that allegiance which is the firft of focial obligations, and the only tie which can hold men together in a Political Union—that it is deftructive of that Loyalty to the Prince, which is the parent of all focial virtues—which ranks next to Religion—and which affords the beft fecurity, not only for the general welfare, but alfo for the performance of the private duties of mankind, in their various relations to each other—in fhort, that fuch a right is exprefly denied by all laws, human and divine—that it is repugnant to uniform experience of mankind in all ages, and that it could not be reduced to practice, without producing all thofe evils which it is the grand object of Society, Government and Laws, to prevent.

But

But to enlarge on thefe topics is unneceffary—Neither can there be any occafion to refute the audacious and treafonable falfhood, that the Sovereign of thefe Realms derives his title from the exercife of fuch a right. The good people of this Country have never exercifed, nor thought themfelves entitled to exercife, fo monftrous a pretenfion. His Majefty fits on the Throne by the Right of Inheritance, and there never was a legal act done refpecting the Crown, which did not recognize that Right. The principles, therefore, which you avowed, were in themfelves principles of Anarchy, Difloyalty, and Rebellion. The doctrine which you maintained is the favourite doctrine of the turbulent and difaffected; and that on which they moft rely to ftir up a fpirit of Infurrection and Revolt.—It is the Fountain Head where all the ftreams of modern fedition and treafon take their rife, and whence they rufh forth to inundate the world, as they have inundated France, with calamity and blood. To promulgate fuch a doctrine in any manner is a high treafonable mifdemeanour;—but to feize fuch an occafion for giving currency to the baneful poifon---to publifh fuch principles in the face of Juftice, folemnly deliberating upon the higheft crime known to the Laws, upon a crime which had itfelf proceeded from the pernicious influence of fuch doctrines---this was, in malignity and mifchief, to furpafs

pafs the guilt imputed to the prifoner. It was the very quinteffence of treafon---it was openly to exhort the difaffected to go on---it was to declare to the band of traitors and confpirators that they were right, that they were authorized to purfue their execrable defigns, and that they fhould never want an advocate, who, in defending their lives, would juftify their atrocities, defy the laws, and brave the juftice of the Country.

Of what value were the profeffions of love and attachment to the perfon of your Sovereign, with which you affected to accompany fuch declarations. Oh infidious love! Oh infulting attachment! Built on no foundation but caprice —and fecured by no fenfe of duty and allegiance. The love of a people for their Prince, like that of a child for its parent, muft be attended with honour, refpect, and veneration—with a fenfe of permanent and indifpenfable duty—any other love than this is fleeting and precarious, and will fubfide, at the voice of a demagogue, into contempt and difobedience.

THE GHOST OF ALFRED.

Nov. 14, 1794.

LETTER II.

To the Hon. THOMAS ERSKINE,

SIR,

THE excellence of Trial by Jury, does not merely confift in the fecurity it affords to every individual that he fhall not be declared guilty, unlefs the charge againft him be eftablifhed according to the regular forms of proceeding, but alfo in the fair and open manner in which it is conducted, and by which it enables the public to form its own opinion upon every cafe that is judicially brought forward. *That* Public, prefent at the Trial, hearing the whole of the evidence, and inveftigating with a fcrutinizing but impartial eye, the minuteft circumftances of the cafe, forms as it were a Court of Appeal from the Verdict of the Jury, and pronounces its own judgment *en dernier refort*. No human authority can enchain the faculties of the mind, or controul the free exercife of opinion. Therefore, although the Verdict of a Jury be entitled to refpect and fubmiffion, as proceeding from lawful and regularly conftituted authority, it cannot

carry

carry conviction to the underftanding, any further than as it may be fupported by the evidence
on which it purports to be founded.

There is, however, no authority too great for
you to affume. You can not only arrogate to
yourfelf the right of the Bench, and dictate the
law to the Jury (as I noticed in my firft Letter);
nay, you are not even content with deciding for
the public upon the propriety of a Verdict—
Thefe are fmall matters for your foaring genius—
you can take upon yourfelf to pronounce for Heaven itfelf, and to anticipate its decrees. Thus,
upon the trial of Mr. Tooke, you obferved to the
Jury, with your accuftomed flippancy, that the
Verdict by which HARDY was acquitted, was recorded in Heaven. That verdict is, indeed, there
recorded; but whether by " the approving fpirit,"
as an earneft of future and open applaufe, as,
with a boldnefs approaching to impiety, you
meant to infinuate—or, as a grofs fpecimen of a
violation of the facred rights of juftice—it is not for
you, to decide.—But this, by way of digreffion.

Great is the utility attending the exercife of
this ulterior and paramount jurifdiction, unfet-
tered by the forms of legal proceedings. It
ftrengthens and confirms that moral influence,
which is, perhaps, ftill more operative than the
fanctions

sanctions of Law, in checking the perpetration
of crimes. It has its use even with respect to
Juries themselves, who, while their Verdicts thus
undergo a revision, are, in a manner, themselves
put upon their Trial; and it must operate as a
beneficial check upon them, to know that their
decisions will be examined, upon the same evidence as came before them, by a discerning public, superior to all influence, and,

Nullius addictus jurare in verba Magistri.

In reviewing the Verdicts of Juries, the public
are ever ready to recognize the humane principle of our Law, that it is better that several
guilty persons should escape, than that one innocent person should suffer. Still, however, it should
not be forgotten that an acquittal, where guilt
has been fully and regularly brought home to the
party accused, is a most serious injury to the
Community. But there are some cases in which
acquittals should be scrutinized with peculiar ex-
actness, and in which, the Juries who pronounce
them are entitled to no favour, if the evidence
be such as to justify conviction. Such are the
cases which may, in their consequences, involve
the safety of the State, and the existence of the
Constitution. On any individual charge of murder or robbery, the evil, though positive, is not
very

very extenfive nor alarming, fhould the guilty be abfolved. But a Treafonable Confpiracy is a direct attack upon the very exiftence of Society, and tends to the deftruction of all Law, Order and Government. It is particularly heinous and aggravated, when, inftead of aiming, merely, like the Treafons of former times, at the life of the individual Prince on the Throne, it takes a broader aim, and feeks the entire fubverfion of the Monarchy, and the total deftruction of that glorious fyftem of political happinefs, which was the flow and gradual acquifition of your anceftors, and which has been tranfmitted to you in a courfe of progreffive improvement through the channel of many revolving centuries. As Treafon is the higheft crime known to the Laws, fo this is the moft atrocious and malignant fpecies of that aggravated offence—

" Treafon
" Moft foul as at the beft it is,
" So this moft foul, bafe and unnatural."

It is the moft dangerous both on account of the guarded and infidious manner in which it advances to the completion of its defigns, and of the total, univerfal and irreparable ruin, which muft attend the attainment of its object. A Jury affembled upon a charge of this nature, may hold in their hands the fate of the Empire and of the Conftitution. The immenfity of the interefts which are then ftaked upon their decifion, calls

upon

upon them in the moſt ſolemn manner to be as cautious not to acquit, if there be ſufficient proof of the charge, as they are ſure to be not to convict, if ſuch proof be not adduced. Humanity itſelf, as well as juſtice and every thing valuable in ſociety, may be wounded, as much by their miſplaced lenity, as by their undue ſeverity. It is not merely the life of the accuſed individual that may depend upon their verdict, but perhaps the lives of all honeſt men, which (as well as *that* of the ſacred Perſonage, ſo juſtly eſteemed by the law of unſpeakably greater value than any other life in the State) are put in imminent danger, if ſuch crimes eſcape with impunity. On ſuch occaſions, Juries ſhould bear in mind, that by the ſame verdict by which they acquit, they may paſs a final ſentence on the Conſtitution.

It is not meant to be ſuggeſted, that upon an accuſation of High Treaſon, even of the dangerous and deſtructive nature above deſcribed, the importance of protecting the Government and of preſerving the State, ſhould ſuperſede the neceſſity of regular forms and of ſatisfactory evidence, in order to juſtify a conviction. The enormity of the offence ſhould only induce an unuſual degree of caution in the Jury, that the guilty (that is, thoſe who

are

are proved to be fo) fhould not efcape. But it fhould be remembered; that on this, as on all other occafions, the imperfection neceffarily attending every procefs of human inveftigation renders it generally impoffible to attain direct, pofitive, and irrefragable proof, or to afcertain the motives and views of human conduct with mathematical certainty. A Jury muft therefore be fatisfied with that reafonable evidence which, according to the nature of the cafe, is the beft that is attainable, although it may not amount to abfolute demonftration. It is very rarely, indeed, that fuch demonftration can be procured ; and the infuperable difficulty of obtaining it has rendered the admiffion of circumftantial evidence indifpenfable in judicial proceedings.

Neither is it meant in this place to pafs either cenfure or approbation on the Verdicts already delivered in fuch of the State Trials as have lately occupied the Tribunals of this Country. Thofe Verdicts are in the judgment of the Public, and will be in the judgment of Pofterity ; but when the fermentation which is now fo ftrong fhall fubfide, it will be more eafy to decide abfolutely on their merits. In the mean time, they are far from deriving any credit from that indecent triumph with which they are received and applauded by that heterogeneous affemblage of factions,

factions, who, difcordant as they are in other refpects, unite in indecently oppofing · the fenfe of the Nation, and who weaken the State by diffentions, at a crifis when its prefervation calls in the ftrongeft manner for the clofeft union. *That* triumph is the moft fcandalous infult. upon the Legiflature of the Country, as well as upon the Grand Jury who found the Bills againft the perfons acquitted : for it implies that thofe refpectable Bodies acted rafhly and op- preffively, as far as they were refpectively inftru- mental in putting the prifoners on their Trial. If this were not the cafe, whatever ground the Verdicts in queftion might afford for calm and rational fatisfaction, they could give none for rapture and exultation.

It is not, however, in the power of thefe Ver- dicts, and ftill lefs of the triumph which fome perfons, under the influence of a fellow-feel- ing, may difplay on the occafion, to raife a doubt in the minds of the Public, as to the propriety of inftituting the Profecutions. Whatever opinion may be entertained refpecting the acquittals, it has been proved beyond all doubt, that the perfons acquitted were far from being lightly put upon their Trial, and that there was *at leaft* fo ftrong a ground of fufpicion againft them, that Government would have moft fcan-

C

daloufly

daloufly neglected its duty, if it had not put their conduct into a courfe of legal invefti-gation.

THE GHOST OF ALFRED.

LETTER

LETTER III.

To the Hon. THOMAS ERSKINE.

SIR,

THE interval that has tranfpired fince the acquittal of your Clients, has been too fhort, and the various feelings excited by thofe acquittals were too lively, for the public opinion, on this fubject, to have as yet fubfided into one uniform and collective fentiment. But whatever difference of opinion may appear to exift, refpecting the acquittals, there is one fact, fo fully, fo clearly and incontrovertibly eftablifhed by the Trials, that an attempt to deny it would involve the groffeft infult on common fenfe, and denote an entire dereliction of all candour and decency. The fact fo eftablifhed is the exiftence of that treafonable Confpiracy, which was the fubject of a Royal Meffage to Parliament—which was confirmed, after the moft attentive inveftigation, by the Reports of the two Houfes—which was made the foundation of an Act of the Legiflature, whereby the immediate prefervation of the State was provided for (as heretofore, in cafes of emer-

gency,)

gency), by a fufpenfion of the Habeas Corpus Act—and which was actually found by the Grand Jury, who put the Prifoners on their Trials.

The exiftence of that Confpiracy has now been fully proved, according to the ftricteft forms of Law, and with all the rigour of judicial inveftigation. The evidence given on the re-cent Trials will remain an eternal memorial on record, in full confirmation of all that has been alledged (and even more) refpecting the reality, the nature, and the alarming ex-tent of fuch a Confpiracy. The moft fcepti-cal have now demonftration within their reach; not by yielding to the impulfe of vague fuf-picion, or to the fuggeftions of general alarm; not even by liftening to the fatherly admo-nition of a gracious and affectionate Prince, nor by attending to the wife and feafonable mea-fures of a vigilant Legiflature; but by pe-rufing a body of proof, regularly brought for-ward in the face of day, and fubmitted to the fevereft fcrutiny of public examination. Nor is it merely by *oral* teftimony, depend-ing on recollection, fubject to partiality, and ca-pable of being depreciated by the unbridled li-cence of forenfic examination, that the *general* charge is fupported; fufficient, amply fufficient

for

for the purpofe, is that *written* evidence, which
came out in fo unqueftionable a fhape, that you
could venture to encounter it only by endeavouring to throw a veil over its moft material parts; which was fubftantiated by docu-
ments found in the poffeffion of the parties accufed; which ftood uncontradicted in every refpect; which could not be fhaken by the
intimidating blufter of a crofs-examination, by
the indifcriminate ufe of invectives and calumny,
by an inceffant outcry againft Spics and In-
formers, by fudden charges and profecutions, haftily raked up to produce a momen-
tary effect, nor by the various other engines
of prejudice, to which, for want of better means
of defence, you were glad to refort, in order to
difcredit the *vivâ voce* witneffes for the Crown.
The *written* evidence was out of the reach
of all your arts and ftratagems; and it is happy
for the caufe of truth, that the Public may
calmly and deliberately weigh that evidence,
remote from the artificial buftle and affected
animation which you know how to introduce,
with all the contrivance of ftage effect, into
the Tribunals of Juftice—and fafe from the influence of that feductive eloquence, which you employ
to bewilder when you cannot hope to convince;
and which, inftead of diffufing an ufeful light, like

C 3   the

the genuine rays of Apollo, exhibits only the
dazzling glare of a meteor, that renders nothing
confpicuous but itfelf, and throws every fur-
rounding object into additional obfcurity.

On fuch folid and immoveable grounds refts
the proof of a Confpiracy, the moft malignant
that ever endangered the fecurity of this or of
any Country---A Confpiracy of a fpecies entirely novel, but infinitely more fubtle in its
nature, more eafy in its progrefs, and more ex-
tenfively ruinous in its tendency, than any of
which former times had a conception---A Confpiracy, invented in the laboratory of the " Rights
of Man ;" formed in the alembic of Modern
Philofophy, upon a complete analyfis of human
nature and of fociety---A Confpiracy, which inftead of advancing directly to its ultimate object,
purfued that object in a circuitous manner, and
endeavoured previoufly to remove every obftacle
to its progrefs by weakening all the focial ties—by
ftimulating into action every corrupt propenfity—
and by converting into a fource of difcontent,
every political inequality, every moral imperfection, every natural evil, and even whatever, by
being exhibited feparately, could be made to
appear difgufting, or be magnified into a defect,
however it might conduce, in its general relation, to the benefit, harmony, and beauty of the
whole

whole fyftem. Having thus prepared a fcheme of mifchief, extenfive as the Country itfelf, and deep as the very foundations of Society, this Confpiracy proceeded in its defigns by means fo artful, and under difguifes fo fpecious, as to be calculated to lull fufpicion even at the very moment of alarm, until the defperate project fhould be advanced too far to be defeated.

The benevolent mind naturally contemplates with complacency every endeavour to ameliorate the condition of humanity ; and the limited extent of the human faculties expofes the bulk of mankind to be fafcinated by propofals that profefs to confult their felicity, and to be induced to think themfelves fufceptible of far greater perfection than Providence has rendered them capable of in the prefent ftate. This was too important and too obvious a truth to efcape the refearch of the modern philofophers, affifted by all the radiance of the new light. Hence the mafk of Reform prefented itfelf as the moft favourable to promote and enfure the fuccefs of the Confpiracy : and although the pernicious publications, which were circulated with indefatigable induftry, and *at a great expence*, in order to poifon the public mind, pointed directly and exprefsly to the entire fubverfion of the fubfifting order of things, and the complete

over-

overthrow of the Conftitution in Church and State ; yet thofe who were employed in that circulation declared, with the moft egregious inconfiftency, that *their* object was Parliamentary Reform,. and *that* by legal and conftitutional means.

It was thus that the well and the ill-difpofed, the virtuous and the vicious, the defigning few and the credulous many, were all embarked in the fame caufe; and the aid of the million was depended on, under the influence of difcontent, to move the vaft machine of Society from its firm and ancient pofition, and to throw it into complete diforder. This plan of operation was not only the moft efficacious, but the moft fecure. At whatever period the Confpiracy might be dragged forward, and made the fubject of judicial enquiry, a defence was always prepared, and that defence was RE-FORM. And numbers who were prevailed upon to engage in the purfuit of that object, confcious of the fincerity of their own profeffions, were difpofed to credit *that* of their coadjutors, and to bear teftimony thereto, in the moft folemn manner, and even under the fanction of an oath. But the Confpiracy had advanced too far, and was evidenced by facts too ftubborn and too unequivocal, to admit of the poffibility of a doubt

refpect-respecting either its existence or its tendency, although individuals might elude justice, by the guarded manner in which their operations had been concerted. The chief promoters of the diabolical plan had adopted a language, and had pursued measures, which demonstrated, in the clearest manner, that the word " Reform" was *a lie in their mouths*. Encouraged by the success of their principles and systems in France, they assumed, in their associated Clubs, the same forms, by which that success had been attained, and which had reduced France into a state of the completest Anarchy. They began a cordial intercourse with the promoters of that Anarchy, and the uniformity of the views of both parties was reciprocally acknowledged. They lost no time in dispatching their Ambassadors to the French Convention, when that body of Traitors had *formally* deposed their KING; and they were advancing with rapid strides, and by all the exertions in their power, to the formation of a *similar* Convention in this Country. The ideas of these persons, respecting the nature and object of a Convention, were sufficiently explained, when the Constitutional Society declared, by a formal Resolution, that the Speech of Citizen ST. ANDRE, (who, together with Citizen BARRERE, was elected an honorary Member) should

be

be inferted in the books of the Society. In that Speech, fo adopted, the Citizen Orator faid, that " the powers of a Convention muft, from " the very nature of the Affembly be *unlimited* " with refpect to every meafure of General " Safety, fuch as THE EXECUTION OF A TY-" RANT. IT IS NO LONGER A CONVENTION, " IF IT HAS NOT POWER TO JUDGE THE " KING." But it would be almoft endlefs, and it is furely unneceffary, to trace throughout, the long and clofely connected chain of evidence, proving that their defign was to effect, under cover of the mafked battery of Reform, the fpeedy and the entire fubverfion of the Monarchy and Conftitution of Great Britain. Suffice it to add, that with the word *Reform* ftill in their mouths, they avowed at length, in plain language, their intention to obtain their object (not, as at firft, by legal and Conftitutional means, but) WITHOUT THE INTERVENTION OF PARLIAMENT, AND IN DEFIANCE OF ITS AUTHORITY. An attempt involving the total fubverfion of Government, and an affumption of its rights; and therefore, according to the clear and undoubted Law of the Land, amounting to the crime of HIGH TREASON.

THE GHOST OF ALFRED.

Nov. 18, 1794.

LETTER

LETTER IV.

To the Hon. *THOMAS ERSKINE.*

SIR,

THE existence of a Treasonable Conspiracy having been fully proved by the evidence adduced during the Trials of some of the individuals charged with that crime, to contend as you have since done in Parliament, that the acquittal of those individuals could destroy, or even diminish the effect of that evidence, is not only to insult, in the grossest manner, the good sense of the Public, but to employ a species of sophistry, which none but the most desperate cause could require. The Verdict of Not Guilty could do no more than decide the fate of the Prisoners, and absolve them from the pains and penalties which the Law attached to the crime with which they were charged: it could not, by the utmost perversion of reason, be made to declare their *moral* innocence in respect of *that* crime; for the only question was, whether their *legal* guilt had been *legally* proved: it did not even *technically* pronounce them

" Not

" Not Guilty" of any thing but High Treaſon,
under the *ſubſiſting* Laws; but left it, not merely
poſſible, but highly probable, that the Juries
thought them guilty of the higheſt poſſible degree of Sedition: and even in the limited ſenſe
of abſolving merely from the *charge* of High
Treaſon, it left the Public at full liberty to form
their own opinion of the propriety of the Verdict.
If this were not the caſe, the mode of Trial by
Jury, inſtead of being a bulwark of Liberty,
would operate as an engine of the moſt grievous
tyranny; as it would fetter and enſlave the operations of the human mind. Who then can poſſeſs the matchleſs effrontery to maintain that the
acquittals, which, in reality, proved ſo little in favour of the individuals delivered thereby from
the legal charge, could diſprove the fact of a
Conſpiracy, which, after having been rendered,
by the peculiar manner in which it was purſued, a
matter of general ſuſpicion and alarm, was at
length completely eſtabliſhed by the moſt deciſive
of all human teſts—a public judicial inveſtiga-
tion ?

So far indeed were the acquittals from con-
tradicting in any reſpect the *general* charge, that
they ſerve, when conſidered in their connection
with all the concomitant circumſtances, even to
corroborate that charge. The exiſtence of a
Con-

Confpiracy was the bafis of the whole proceeding. It was the neceffary foundation of the
cafe for the profecution. If this ground-work
had not been laid in the moft folid manner, and
fo as to preclude all doubt, can it be fuppofed
that the Prifoners would have been put upon
their defence? What had they to defend themfelves againft, if no crime had been proved?
Would the ATTORNEY GENERAL, finding that
the very foundations of his cafe had failed him,
have proceeded upon a bafelefs profecution? If
fo, he would not have merited thofe compli-
ments for candour and liberality, which you fo
profufely beftowed upon him. Or if he had fhewn
himfelf difpofed to perfift, after the evidence for
the profecution had left the truth of the general
charge, the reality of the Confpiracy, on vague
and precarious grounds, what became at that
moment of the Counfel for the Prifoners? How
did they acquit themfelves of the duty they had
undertaken? Did they rife and fubmit to the
Court, that *in their apprehenfion no cafe had
been made out which could require any anfwer
from their Clients; that the evidence for the
Crown had failed to eftablifh the exiftence of the
Confpiracy, which was the offence charged, and
the neceffary ground-work of the profecution;
that if the fhadow of a doubt could remain, at
that ftage of the proceeding, not merely of the
fact,*

fact, but of the legal, regular, and unanswer-
able proof of the crime, it could answer no pur-
pose,· but that of trifling with the solemnities of
justice, to proceed any further ; for that, in such
a case, an acquittal must necessarily ensue, as it
could not be supposed that the defence would sup-
ply the deficiency of the prosecution, in establishing
the charge, and the Jury could never convict,
unless they were convinced both of the truth of
that charge, and of its particular application to
the persons accused ; and that, therefore, they
(the Counsel) demanded, as of right, an immediate
acquittal ? On the ftrange neglect of the Counfel
to urge fuch reafoning, which, in the cafe fuppofed, would have been unanfwerable, would not
the Judge have been bound to interfere, and to
have put it to the Jury, that, if they difbelieved,
after what they had heard, the exiftence of any
Confpiracy to fubvert the Monarchy, and to depofe the King from his legal and conftitutional
dignity (which was the crime charged in the
Indictment), they could never confcientioufly
convict the Prifoners ; that if the evidence for the
Profecution was clofed without having eftabliifhed,
to the fatisfaction of the Jury, fo effential a pre-
liminary, there was no cafe made out which required any anfwer; and that therefore it was to
no purpofe to call upon the Prifoners for a defence againft a charge, already too weak to juftify

tify a conviction. If, however, the Judge had
unaccountably omitted fuch an interference,
would not the Jury have fuggefted to the Bench
their doubt of the exiftence of the Confpiracy,
if fuch a doubt had been entertained by them ;
would they not have enquired whether, according to the forms of proceeding, that doubt was
likely to be removed in the fubfequent ftages of
the Trial ; and if not, whether as it muft ulti-
mately lead to an acquittal, they might not as
well pronounce that acquittal without further
delay ? Do you imagine that their impatience
to liften to the ftrains of your eloquence, and
their eagernefs to fee your powers of reafoning
exerted in defending your Clients from a charge,
which had not been proved even in the *abftract*,
would have made them reject fo fair an occafion
of obtaining a releafe from the moft haraffing fervice in which Jurymen had ever been engaged, and
of being reftored to their homes and their families ?
But if, notwithftanding all thefe various opportunities of cutting fhort the Trials, the dignity
of a Tribunal of Criminal Juftice had been pro-
ftituted to the ridiculous farce of putting the parties accufed upon their defence, againft a charge,
which had not been proved to have any exiftence, except on the face of the Indictment ; if
you, unmindful of fo fundamental a defect in
the cafe for the profecution, thought proper to

wafte

.wafte your talents in making a moft elaborate defence to that charge; if you ftill felt and acknowledged the immenfe difficulty of the tafk you
had undertaken, and collected all your refources
of art and ability to move the paffions of the
Jurymen, left you might fail to convince their
reafon.; how is it to be explained that thofe Jurymen, exhaufted as they were, fhould, in two
out of the three cafes which they tried, have
hefitated fo long in pronouncing Verdicts of
acquittal, if they really difbelieved the fact of a
Confpiracy? If their Verdicts had been founded
on a difbelief of that fact, rather than on a doubt
of its being brought legally home to the accufed
perfons, they could have had no occafion to hefitate for five minutes: nay, as in confequence
of the unprecedented length of the Trials, they
had repeated opportunities for mutual conference,
even after all the evidence to prove the Confpiracy which had been given, they would probably have been ready to fay, " Not Guilty,"
without even going out of Court. Upon a
profecution for murder, would the Jury retire or hefitate one moment to acquit, if they
were convinced that no murder had been committed. The time that either of the Juries
was out of Court, appeared to the Public
extremely fhort to determine upon an acquittal, againft fuch a weight of evidence, and
on

on so very serious a charge : but that time, or even a hundredth part of it, was entirely unnecessary, to enable the Jury to agree upon an acquittal, if the foundation of the charge had not been laid, by satisfactory proof of the existence of the Conspiracy. Even the single circumstance, that the Jury who tried the Rev. JOHN HORNE TOOKE, made up their minds in ten minutes to acquit, when the two other Juries were, one near two, and the other above three hours, in forming the same resolution, notwithstanding that the proof of the Conspiracy was the same in all, demonstrates that the only question with the Juries, was the application of the charge to the respective Prisoners, and that no doubt existed as to the fact of the crime. (It will be remembered, that the evidence respecting the project of a Convention, was not brought home to Mr. TOOKE,—whether in consequence of his superior caution and sagacity, or because he was not privy or assenting to that project, I will not pretend to determine.) But if, after all, it had been established, as the result of the trials, that the idea of a Conspiracy turned out upon examination to be a groundless fiction, unsupported by proof, as well as destitute of probability (as some persons have the audacity to assert), how happens it that your Clients have neither brought, nor even threatened to bring, their actions at

D   law

law for falſe impriſonment, againſt the Miniſters of the Crown, who committed them for trial? You well know, that unleſs it could be made to appear that there were *very ſolid grounds* for the commitments, and for the proſecutions which followed, there are *very ſolid grounds*, to entitle the parties to heavy damages. It will ſcarcely be believed that an unwillingneſs to harraſs the Executive Government, and to embarraſs it's operations, at the moſt critical junčture this Country ever knew, reſtrains you from adviſing ſuch ačtions, or your Clients from taking that advice. You dare not, however, make the experiment : and, in refraining from it, you furniſh a *damning* proof of THE REAL EXISTENCE OF THE CONSPIRACY.

It appears, then, that the verdičts of acquittal which terminated the late proſecutions for High Treaſon, were perfečtly conſiſtent with the deciſive proof which the Trials had afforded of the exiſtence of a Treaſonable Conſpiracy, and that thoſe Verdičts, when conſidered in their general connečtion with the whole of the proceedings, far from diminiſhing in any degree the force of that proof, did in ſome reſpečts even confirm and ſtrengthen it. That being the caſe, it would ſurely be too much for any one to contend that the acquittals could leſſen the danger which at all times, and eſpecially

especially at a time like the present, must be inseparable from such a Conspiracy. The glaring absurdity of such an assertion must preserve every one from the folly of making it. If the Trials established the existence of the crime, the acquittals announced the escape of the Criminals; and that equally, whether the parties accused were innocent or guilty; for if they were innocent, the acquittals proved that the Criminals had eluded DISCOVERY—if guilty, that they had eluded JUSTICE. In either case, and there is no alternative, the danger is increased, and the necessity of vigilance and precaution is increased also.

Without passing any judgment on the propriety of the Verdicts of " Not Guilty," and supposing even that honest and conscientious men could not have pronounced different Verdicts, it is, nevertheless, undoubtedly true, that guilt has hitherto escaped, and that Treason has triumphed over the Laws, although, thank Heaven, it has not yet triumphed over the Constitution.

The security of the Constitution has, however, been considerably diminished. Either from a defect in the Laws, or from some other cause, the forms of Justice have proved adequate only to substantiate the offence, but not to punish the

offenders.

offenders. The greateft of all poffible crimes, attended with the higheft degree of aggravation, has been proved, by legal evidence, beyond the poffibility of a doubt; a Confpiracy, not merely to wreft the fceptre from the reigning Monarch, but to "TEAR UP THE MONARCHY BY THE ROOTS," to annihilate for ever the Conftitution, and, in direct and avowed imitation of the fuccefsful example of France, to introduce a fyftem of complete anarchy. Such a Confpiracy, long evidenced by fymptoms which filled every honeft breaft with anxiety, and purfued with fo much art that the means of fuccefs were thofe of defence alfo—fuch a Confpiracy, fo malignant, fo fubtle, and fo deftructive, has been regularly fubmitted to the Tribunals of Juftice, it has been incontrovertibly eftablifhed, and the refult has fhewn that the Conftitution is deftitute of the protection of the Laws. The fource of all focial fecurity, the terror of Juftice, has failed the Conftitution at the moment of danger, and has left it expofed to the affaults of its enemies. The mounds and the barriers which have hitherto fufficed for its protection, have been found infufficient to withftand the novel fpecies of attack, invented by the profeffors of modern philofophy and the " RIGHTS OF MAN :" as the fortifications of ancient times, which could refift the

catapult

catapult and the battering ram, would furnish no defence against the thunder of modern artillery.

The acquittals, therefore, far from diminishing the danger, of which the spontaneous feelings of every man had informed him, may be considered, without any imputation either on the Juries or even on the persons accused, to be subjects of the justest alarm.—Their obvious tendency is to impress the minds of the people at large with an idea of the weakness of the Laws, and of the immense, and almost insuperable difficulties, which Justice has to encounter, in order to detect and punish the worst of criminals. Their natural effect is to weaken the bands of society, by diminishing the respect of the people for Government ; (the unavoidable consequence of its being made to appear that Government may be attacked with impunity.) The depraved, the turbulent, and the seditious, will, of course, be rendered more daring and presumptuous, when they find that the most desperate attempts, to destroy for ever the peace and order of society, are attended with so little hazard. Every Conspirator and Incendiary in the kingdom takes courage from the result of the prosecutions, the institution of which filled him with dismay, and considers every acquittal as a pledge for his own impunity, provided he keep within the bounds

prescribed

preſcribed. The newly diſcovered courſe of
Treaſon has now been clearly delineated—it has
been ſhewn to be ſafe from perils—to be free
from rocks, ſhoals, and quickſands—to be ſecure,
AS THE LAW NOW STANDS, from Juſtice,
and to require nothing but patient perſeve-
rance, (avoiding only any deviation into another
tract,) in order to conduct, ſafely and proſperouſly,
to its ultimate deſtination, THE COMPLETE
OVERTHROW OF THE STATE AND CONSTITU-
TION.

THE GHOST OF ALFRED.

Jan. 20, 1795.

LETTER

LETTER V.

To the Right Hon. CHARLES JAMES FOX.

SIR,

THE truly honeft and confcientious man is as incapable of an attempt to miflead the judgment, as to invade the rights of property. He would as foon commit a robbery, as be guilty of intentional fophiftry ; nay, as practical truth is, in his eftimation, of infinitely more value than gold, he would feel even more repugnance to deceive than to fteal; but of all poffible crimes, there is not one which he holds in greater abhorrence than the wilful perverfion of truth and of reafon, on matters which involve the welfare of States and the aggregate happinefs of millions;—which engage the moft folemn difcuffion in Senates, and excite deliberation of Legiflatures. On thefe fubjects, to make the worfe appear the better reafon, at the rifk of all the confequences which may attend the fuccefs of fophiftry and the prevalence of error, is the quinteffence of vice, and the utmoft extreme of human depravity.

D 4

It

It is a melancholy proof of the corruption of modern times, that the above criminal practice is grown so habitual, as to be pursued in utter defiance of all decency; while the men who are notorious for such a conduct, instead of being holden in the contempt and detestation which they deserve, and which would render them almost innocuous, are enabled to effect their mischievous purposes, by being permitted, at all times, and to any extent, to command the public attention. Nothing can be a stronger proof that the public feelings are destitute of that sensibility which is the best preservative of virtue; nor can any symptom indicate more forcibly that the country touches upon its fate. The mere frequency of such a spectacle is alone sufficient to corrupt the taste of a Nation, and to vitiate its principles.

> " Vice is a monster of so frightful mien,
> " As to be hated, needs but to be seen;
> " But seen too oft, familiar with her face,
> " We first endure, then pity, then embrace."

And yet every day is the atrocious spectacle repeated—Every day witnesses the scandalous and immoral exhibition of a set of men, possessing public consequence, but entirely destitute of public principle, who openly prostitute their talents to the perversion of reason and the sacrifice of truth and consistency; who employ the political character

character with which they are unworthily in-
vested, in unceafing endeavours to miflead the
.public mind, to obftruct public bufinefs, to
create general difcontent and difunion, to fruf-
trate every plan of utility, and even every meafure of neceffary defence, and to embarrafs
the Government, although, on the fuccefs of its
exertions, depends the falvation of the Country. The oppofition of thefe men is fyftematic—
they indifcriminately refift whatever is propofed,
with this difference only, that in proportion as it
is excellent and important, their refiftance is
diftinguifhed by virulence and obftinacy. Their
motives are compounded in various degrees of
perfonal ambition and perfonal animofity, but the
former generally predominates, and rather than
forego its gratification, they make no fcruple to
endanger the very exiftence of the State. The
object they invariably purfue is, by the aid of ca-
vil, mifreprefentation and artificial odium, to deprive Adminiftration of that public confidence
and fupport without which it cannot act with vi-
gour and effect—with a view of afcribing the
failure of its meafures to its own demerits and
infufficiency. Not even a ftate of War can roufe
the patriotifm of thefe men : on the contrary,
as it furnifhes them with additional opportunities, fo it operates by way of additional incite-
ment, to purfue their defperate projects. The
mifconftruction to which fuch a fituation gives
occafion,

occasion, the difficulties, viciffitudes, and difasters
to which it is expofed, the burdens, hardfhips,
and calamities which unavoidably attend its con-
tinuance, and the impatience natural to the human mind to exchange fo irkfome a condition for
that of peace and repofe—thefe, and a variety of
other circumftances, render a ftate of War the
harveft of an unprincipled Oppofition. No
matter that the arms of the Country fhould
be unfuccefsful for want of internal energy
and union; no matter that the honour of
the Nation fhould be tarnifhed, and that it
fhould be reduced at laft to depend for its fecurity, and perhaps its exiftence, on an inglorious
and unfubftantial Peace—No matter that the
Conftitution fhould be expofed to deftruction
by the eftablifhment of a fyftem of Anarchy, which feeks to overwhelm all regular Government, and which has already convulfed civilized fociety to its very foundations—Thefe confiderations are of no moment, compared to the
grand and indifpenfable object—the expulfion
of a Minifter. Better that the ftate veffel
fhould perifh than be preferved by a rival at the
helm.

Nothing can exceed the mifchievous effects
produced by an Oppofition acting on fuch principles. Suppofing that it fhould fail to involve
the

the Country in total and immediate ruin, which, at a crifis like the prefent, is its direct tendency, it impairs the beneficial energies of Government, and perverts the fpirit of the Conftitution. It converts thofe principles of check and controul, which were intended to preferve the balance and the harmony of the political fyftem, into clogs and obftructions. It is the real fource of corrupt influence, which it renders neceffary, in order to prevent the machine from being totally impeded by the hindrance thus interpofed. It deprives the Country of the advantages it might derive from the watchfulnefs of an honeft and confcientious Oppofition, whofe juft and difcriminating cenfures would afford a real fecurity againft the fupinenefs, inaptitude or depravity of an Adminiftration. It almoft nullifies the principle of refponfibility, which the Conftitution attaches to the fituation of Minifters; for, by the artificial embarraffment it creates, it deprives their meafures of that freedom of operation, and of that chance for fuccefs, without which it would be the higheft injuftice to make them ftrictly accountable; and it furnifhes them, at the fame time, with an excufe for failure, and with a pretence for fhifting the blame from themfelves (even where it may belong to them), which they certainly ought not to poffefs. Of this, indeed, the Oppofition are fo confcious, that they never pur-

fue

sue a Minister beyond the confines of his office.
When once they have driven him to that bourn
of obscurity and oblivion, from whence they hope
he will never return, their resentments instantly
cease; then animosities are appeased; their threats
of "*axes*" and "*scaffolds*" die away. They regard
him as politically defunct, and seem to lose all recollection of his transgressions.--Whether this
proceed from some latent spark of conscience,
which will not permit them to pursue others to
punishment for sins *really* their own; or, from
prudential motives, which warn them not to in-
stitute an enquiry, in which they may themselves
be so deeply involved; or from a persuasion that
the loss of office is complete an expiation for
the greatest offences, as intirely to wash away
the stain of guilt, to regenerate the delinquent,
and qualify him for confidence and *coalition* with
the purest characters; from which of these causes
foever it happens that the success of Opposition is
crowned with forbearance, your own experience
and recollection can, better than any other man's,
inform you.

But the baneful effects of an Opposition conducted in the manner above described, are not
confined to the obstruction of the benefits which
the Constitution is calculated to bestow, they also
extend to the destruction of its essence. They

confound

confound the boundaries of its component parts, by caufing thofe parts to encroach on each other, and they fet the theory and the practice of the Conftitution at variance. Hence it is that the Executive Power is fo cramped in the exercife of all its Prerogatives, that an uninformed obferver, judging merely from appearances, would fuppofe thofe Prerogatives to be vefted in Parliament rather than in the Crown, or at leaft, though belonging to the latter, that they are unaccompanied with efficiency. This is owing to the pertinacity with which Oppofition are inceffantly enforcing, on all occafions, that right of interference, which is indeed the privilege of Parliament, but which is intended by the Conftitution only to be exercifed on particular occafions, and for particular purpofes. Nay, to fuch an extent is this interference carried, that under the infidious cover of a fictitious fubftitution of the Minifter in the place of his Mafter, that refpect which is due to the Sovereign, and which is fo effential to the happinefs of the People, is violated in the groffeft manner, by a factious and fcurrilous Party. The important Prerogative of War and Peace, by which the Crown is made the conftitutional confervator of the honour and of the political interefts of the Nation, is fo manacled, as to be deprived of its efficacy, and reduced nearly to a cypher. Every form of Parliament, every

pri-

privilege of the subject, (not excepting the important right of petitioning) is converted into an impediment to the free, vigorous and beneficial exercise of that Prerogative. And although a War may have been commenced under an universal conviction of its justice and necessity—although it may have had the firmest concurrence of Parliament, in its *constitutional* character, as entitled to vote or to refuse the supplies for its pro·secution—yet so many obstacles are thrown in its way, that the Country, divided by the cavils of an unprincipled Opposition, has not a fair chance of success. Every circumstance of difficulty or delay, every occurrence of check or disaster, every additional burthen or inconvenience, is taken advantage of, to damp the spirit of the Nation, and to drive still further the wedge of division: until the Executive Power, embarrassed still more by the hydra of domestic Faction, than by the force of the foreign Enemy, finds it impossible to continue the War with that steady perseverance and effect, which are necessary to the attainment of an honourable and substantial Peace.

Nor are the malignant and mischievous efforts of Party confined to ordinary Wars, undertaken in support of partial though important interests, and which may admit of secure pacification with the

the Enemy, even though their object should be found to be unattainable: those efforts are pursued with as much acrimony as ever, even now, that the Country is engaged in a War, on the success of which depends the existence, not merely of the British Empire, but of Civil Society. In direct breach of the most express assurances of support, the desperate band of opposition, as incapable of fidelity as of every public virtue, resist, with inextinguishable and increasing rancour, all the endeavours of Government to bring this War to a prosperous issue. Instead of setting an example of unanimity, so necessary at such a crisis, they hold up the torch of discord, and convert every motive of coherence into a source of dissention. They endeavour, by their perverse reasonings, by their incessant interruptions, by their vexatious enquiries, by their captious charges, and by all the arts of misrepresentation, to give the clue to Faction, to impede the exertions of the Country, and to withdraw the confidence and affection of the People from Government. They are constantly labouring to excite the despondency of the timid, to stimulate the machinations of the evil-disposed, and to blunt that abhorrence and indignation, with which the principles and conduct of the Enemy must inspire every virtuous breast. And although they are prevented by a vast majority of honest Senators, from attaining their avowed object of throw-

ing

ing the Nation at once at the feet of its perfidious adverfary, they hope, by dint of perfeverance, to fucceed at laft, in rendering the bulk of the People adverfe to a War, of which the ftrenuous profecution affords the laft defence of Property, of Religion, and of every thing defervedly dear or valuable to man.

But, in order to do complete juftice to the Party to which the above obfervations refer, and of which, to your indelible difgrace, you are the acknowledged Leader, it is neceffary to view the conduct of that Party on the occafion of the Treafonable Confpiracy, which has been recently formed againft the Government of this Country; which, but for the wife and timely precautions of Parliament, would, ere now, have laid the Conftitution in ruins; and which has been rendered even more dangerous by the impunity of its contrivers and abettors. But, the peculiar importance of this fubject entitles it to diftinct confideration.

THE GHOST OF ALFRED

March 5, 1795.

LETTER

LETTER VI.

Sir,

THAT the French Revolution was the focus of a deep and vast conspiracy against all the ancient institutions of Europe, civil, political, and religious, is a truth which is now become so notorious, that an attempt to illustrate it, would be an insult on the senses of mankind. The germ of this conspiracy was that licentious and infidel system which has for many years been propagated by a set of men generally denominated modern *philosophers*---A system which has for its object to eradicate from the human mind all those sentiments and principles, which constitute or strengthen the bond of social union, and to inculcate notions of wild and incoherent rights, which have never yet existed in practice, and which are incompatible with the existence of society. This system, meeting in France with a light, frivolous, and corrupted people, and with a Prince of a weak and indecisive character, in the twinkling of an eye overthrew a Monarchy which had existed for fourteen centuries, and which was considered as the most potent and solid Govern-

E   ment

ment of Europe, and with it, every establishment, human or divine, which had conduced to the order or stability of the State.

But it was not to France alone that the abettors of this system confined their views. On the contrary, they did not hesitate to declare openly, that their scheme of Philanthropy, as they termed it, *embraced the whole world**. The astonishing success of the first experiment could not fail to encourage them to pursue their avowed object of universal Revolution; and, indeed, the fires they had lighted in France must soon have burnt out, unless supplied with fuel from other countries. Hence the French Revolutionists immediately turned their thoughts to the extension of the mischief. They lost no time in dispatching their emissaries, in all directions, to disseminate or expand those principles which, when fully put in

---

* On the 14th Dec. 1792, one of the Members of the Convention thus recalled to the recollection of his Audience the means which had been employed by the first promoters of the Revolution to disseminate its principles. " Call to mind (said he) those days when Petion, Condorcet, Syeyes, &c. surrounded in the Pantheon like the Grecian Philosophers at Athens, instructed a multitude of disciples, making them perceive in our Decrees, THE SEEDS OF GENERAL INSURRECTION ; that these strangers might disseminate the same seeds in their respective Countries, and PRODUCE SIMILAR REVOLUTIONS THROUGHOUT THE WORLD."

action,

action, had been proved to be irrefiftible; they paffed decrees, openly inviting the people of every country to infurrection; and they reforted to War, with a view not only of eftablifhing their own ufurped authority, but of affifting the dif-affected of other States, in the fubverfion of their lawful Governments.

The liberty enjoyed in this Country afforded, for a time, an unbounded fcope to the machinations of the French emiffaries and their coadjutors. The prefs was moft affiduoufly employed in circulating the fubtle, but potent poifon, to every part of the body politic. The feditious were congregated in Clubs, in order not merely to combine their own exertions, but to afford a ren-dezvous to the reftlefs, the profligate and the difaffected, and to all who, from whatever motive, were defirous of a change.

Thefe Clubs, ramified by means of *affiliations*, were fpreading over the whole extent of the Country; and their members were every where engaged in circulating the moft infamous libels on the Conftitution, in endeavouring to alienate the affections of the people from their Govern-ment, and in recommending the French Revo-lution to their imitation.

The horrid 10th of Auguft, which completed the overthrow of the Gallic Throne, gave the fignal to the Englifh confpirators, who inftantly proceeded openly to difplay their real defigns. They fent their congratulations to the French Convention, on the occafion of the King's depofition, and thereby they put it beyond the poffibility of a doubt, that the object of the Convention, which they were endeavouring to form, was the depofition of the Britifh Monarch.

At this moment, the crifis feemed to be faft approaching. The horizon was every where involved in the deepeft gloom, and the fky was overfpread with clouds of the moft portentous afpect. Alarm filled the breafts not only of thofe who had long obferved the growing danger, but even of thofe who had been hitherto ftrangers to fear. Confternation was vifible in the faces of all who did not aim at the overthrow of the Conftitution; excepting, indeed, a fmall, but defperate band, who were determined to rifk every thing, rather than abandon their factious views. Thofe who were confpiring to effect the ruin of their Country, difplayed the utmoft confidence and exultation. The ftorm was ready to burft, when the Country was providentially faved by the inftantaneous union of the friends of the Conftitution, who formed themfelves into loyal Affociations, *for the protection of liberty and pro-*

perty

perty against republicans and levellers. This
sudden and general combination, which nothing
but an instinctive and universal sense of extreme
danger could have produced, astonished the agents
of sedition; who, far from calculating upon such
a resistance, had imagined that all concert and
union would here, as in France, have been
confined to themselves; and, as they knew that
the unsuspecting and unconnected many are
easily kept in awe by the desperate and closely-
united few, prepared for every emergency, and
aided by the turbulent, profligate and abandoned,
of every description, they expected an easy triumph
over a Government unsupported by the people.

But, at the sight of the Associations, the
Conspirators, in their turn, stood aghast---When
they were almost ready to shout victory, they
skulked to their lurking holes; and, for a moment, they seemed to renounce their desperate
projects. Soon, however, they endeavoured to
resume their activity; but, awed by the check
they had received, they assumed an artful disguise, and sought to conceal their ultimate designs
under the mask of reform. At length, they made
another attempt to form a Convention, which,
under the pretext of Parliamentary reform, was to
supersede Parliament, and to usurp all the
powers of Government. But while they were preparing for an explosion, their deliberations were

seasonably

feafonably interrupted by the vigilance of Government. The leaders were put upon their trial to anfwer facts which both Houfes of Parliament, in the moft folemn manner, afferted to be true, and which a Grand Jury charged upon their oaths.--- The fequel is but too well known.

Thus the Confpiracy in this Country, which happily has been detected and fruftrated, but which unhappily has not yet been punifhed, was but a branch of that great Confpiracy which the French Revolutionifts had formed againft all the Governments of Europe. Its fuccefs has hitherto been prevented by the union of the people, and the energy of the Government. May neither relax their efforts; for the danger will never ceafe while the Republic of France fhall continue to exift. While that inexhauftible fource of Revolutions fhall remain open, there will be no fafety for any Government upon earth.

The conduct of yourfelf and the party of which you are the avowed head, during the progrefs of thefe awful events, exhibits a fpecimen of political and moral depravity not to be equalled in the annals of faction. The French Revolution had long affumed a decided character of confifcation, maffacre and treafon, and it threatened to become the fcourge of mankind, when, in the moft public and folemn manner, you pronounced

. it.

it to be *the moſt glorious edifice of liberty, which
had been erected on the foundation of human in-
tegrity in any age or country.*

Confiſtently with this declaration, you have
made the French Revolution the theme of your
conſtant panegyric--you have adopted and avowed
its principles- -you have declared for the holy right
of inſurrection---and, not content with aſſerting
the Sovereignty of the People, and their right to
rebel, you have audaciouſly and treaſonably pre-
ſumed to trace the title of your ſovereign to that
ſource *. You have juſtified the crimes of the
Revolu-

* On the 1ſt of February, 1793, Mr. Fox is reported to
have uſed, in the Houſe of Commons, the following language, which has never been diſavowed by him : " The
" people are the Sovereigns in all countries—they may
" amend, alter and aboliſh the form of Government under
" which they live, at pleaſure—they may caſhier their
" Monarchs for miſconduct. James the Second was caſhiered.
" The people elected William. They elected the Houſe of
" Brunſwick, even the whole dynaſty. It is clear, therefore,
" that the preſent family enjoy the Throne from the Sove-
" reignty of the People." And on the 13th December,
1792, he ſaid, in the ſame place, " The right of the Houſe
" of Brunſwick to the Throne originated in the only genuine
" fountain of all Royal Power, THE WILL OF THE MANY."
Of ſuch language, the mildeſt thing that can be ſaid, is,
that its object ſeems to be to recommend and enforce French
Jacobinical principles, by means of an infamous libel on the
title of the Sovereign, as well as on the Conſtitution, which,
as Mr. Fox well knows, never did, either in principle or in
praⁿⁱⁱ

Revolution. You have not only applauded the revolts, mutinies, and treafons, by which it was effected, but you have recommended them to the example of other Countries*. You have palliated even its moft fhocking atrocities ; and you have exulted in thofe victories by which France has reduced a great part of Europe to flavery.

In like manner you have patronized the caufe and encouraged the efforts of thofe who fought to introduce French revolutionary principles and practices into this Country. With what zeal have you ftood forward in Parliament to dif-countenance every endeavour to check the circu-lation of their baneful poifon---With what affi-duity have you laboured to prevent any reftraints being impofed on the unbounded licentioufnefs of the Prefs. When the Clubs and Societies, which correfponded with French Traitors, confpired the fubverfion of the Englifh Government, with what ardour did you undertake their defence, and contend againft any interruption of their pro-

practice, recognize any thing like an elective title to the Throne, and which, in the cafe of the Revolution, affords the ftrongeft poffible proof that it abhors all idea of fuch a title.

* On the 9th February, 1790, Mr. Fox is alfo reported to have faid that " the French army, by refufing to obey the " dictates of the Court," (that is, the commands of their lawful Sovereign) " had fet a glorious example to all the " military of Europe."

ceedings---

ceedings---And when the great body of loyal fubjects affociated for the prefervation of the Conftitution, and in fupport of the Laws, with what
acrimony did you abufe and vilify them! At
length, when a gang of Confpirators were feized
in the very act of framing a Convention, which
was to affume the entire authority of Government, and which, according to the language of
their own papers, would not be a Convention
unlefs it had power *to judge the King, and to
execute a Tyrant*, with what indignation did you
refent---with what zeal did you oppofe every
endeavour to enforce the laws againft fuch flagitious criminals, and with what indecent triumph did you exult at their efcape from juftice.
But what fhall be faid of your conduct when Parliament, in its wifdom, judged it neceffary to encounter, by new Laws, the fubtle wiles of French
Revolutionary Treafon, which had eluded the
operation of the ancient Statutes? Hiftory will
record the fpeech by which you founded the
Trumpet of Infurrection, when you found, that,
in fpite of all your endeavours to provide for
the *future* impunity of Traitors, the Bills which
you oppofed were likely to pafs. Pofterity, however, will fcarcely believe, that a man could be
found in Parliament fo wicked as to declare, that,
becaufe the Legiflature felt the neceffity of
providing additional fecurity for the Perfon of
the Sovereign, and for the prefervation of the
Con-

Conftitution, all ties of allegiance—all obligations
of duty and fubmiffion—were diffolved; and
that refiftance was become *a queftion---not of
morality, but of prudence**.

Upon the whole, fuch has been the countenance
and encouragement which you. have afforded to
the internal and external enemies of your Country,
that the perfeverance of both in their execrable
and deftructive defigns, may, without any exag-
geration, be afcribed to the hopes which your
language and conduct have led them to form.

---

* A late fpeech attributed to Mr. Fox feems to be a direct
attempt to make a *practical* application of this doctrine. He
is reported at a late meeting of the Whig Club (which it
fhould be remembered is now nothing lefs than a foul mixture of Faction and Jacobinifm) after giving as his toaft,
" The Sovereignty of the People," to have expreffed a hope
that the Affociations which are now forming for the defence
of the Country, would, after averting a foreign yoke, employ their arms for " the dethroning of *Domeftic Tyrants.*" Such
language can require no comment; but furely it ought to
infpire Government with the greateft caution, left, in giving
prudent encouragement to the noble and martial fpirit which
is now difplayed throughout the country, it fhould afford
an opportunity to the perfons on whom Mr. Fox muft be
fuppofed to rely, for the hellifh purpofe expreffed in his
fpeech, to render themfelves formidable by the acquifition of
arms. It is an immenfe machine which is now forming.
May it never become ungovernable !—*Editor's Note.*

Without

Without the support of a party in Parliament, the domestic traitors would never, with any degree of confidence, have persisted in their endeavours to overturn the Constitution---And, without their encouraging assurances and sanguine invitations, the foreign enemy would, in all probability, have refrained from an attack, which had for its immediate object to favour the progress of insurrection. Thus may the growth of Treason, and the breaking out of the War, be fairly laid to your charge.

Should conscience ever resume her functions in your breast, your situation will be dreadful beyond description. The sufferings which a mind like yours must then experience, would almost excite pity in the heart of a Jacobin. And yet a feeling of benevolence impels me to wish that you may undergo those expurgatory sufferings, rather than that you should be sent " to your account" with all your transgressions " on your head."

THE GHOST OF ALFRED.

May 20, 1795.

LETTER

LETTER VII.

To the Right Hon. CHARLES JAMES FOX.

SIR,

THE attempt made by yourfelf and your political Affociates to deny the exiftence of that treafonable confpiracy, which has lately been the fubject, both of legiflative interference and judicial inveftigation, denotes *that* total difregard for public opinion which accompanies only the utmoft degree of profligacy, and evinces, not merely the confcioufnefs of a total lofs of reputation, but an indifference to character, of which none but the moft abandoned are capable. When principle is extinct, there often furvives a fenfe of fhame, which preferves at leaft an appearance of decency; and which, although it cannot amend the heart, poffeffes an happy influence over the conduct. But thofe dregs of Party, with which you continue to mix, and which, to the difgrace of former Parties of that defcription, ftill retain the title of *Oppofition*, are as infenfible to fhame as they are to virtue, and knowing their character to be defperate and ir-

retriev-

retrievable, they renounce, without a blush, and without a figh, the possibility of ever posseffing the esteem or confidence of their Country.

The ground, on which you pretend to controvert the charge of the Conspiracy, will be found, upon examination, not only to expose the infincerity of your reasoning, and the fallacy of your conclusion, but also to involve a principle of the most dangerous kind; a principle, which clearly evinces that you have no true regard for Trial by Jury, and that you either do not know in what its real excellence confifts, or do not fcruple, to facrifice, for the purpofes of faction, all the advantages refulting from that inftitution. Inftead of referring to the facts and circumftances, in which the Confpiracy was alledged to confift, in order to fhew that the charge was unfounded, you cautioufly avoid fuch a reference, and without venturing to touch upon any part of the complicated hiftory of the Confpiracy, you infer the non-exiftence of the crime from the fingle circumftance of the acquittal of the perfons accufed. Had it been poffible to find any thing in the *cafe* which would have warranted your conclufion, can it be fuppofed that inftead of availing yourfelf of fuch an advantage, you would have relied folely upon a *Verdict* to fupport an
                                                            opinion

opinion which is at direct variance with the decided sentiments of the public ?

It muft, however, be admitted, that on this
occafion you and your Party are perfectly con-
fiftent with yourfelves, and that you adhere
clofely to your ufual mode of proceeding:
Whoever will take the trouble to examine your
reafonings, will find that they are founded upon
the perverfion of whatever is fufceptible of ambiguity, and the fuppreffion of what is clear
and unequivocal. The ambiguity of a general
verdict of " Not Guilty," rendered it precifely
fuch an argument as you are accuftomed to employ. A Delphic Oracle could not have fuited
your purpofe better. Its being abfolutely in-
conclufive of the point in queftion, was amply
fufficient to induce you to reprefent it as conclufive in your favour. Such are the topics to
which you conftantly refort, and which, by
long practice, you know perfectly well how to
mould to your defign; and by their aid, though
you cannot hope to convince, you fucceed but
too frequently in your endeavours to perplex and
confound.

Without adverting at prefent to the monftrous
abfurdity of inferring the non-exiftence of the
crime from the acquittal of the party accufed,

your

your doctrine that *an acquittal is a complete establishment of innocence* is no lefs pernicious in its
tendency, than fallacious in principle. Such a doctrine is incompatible with the mild fpirit of Englifh
criminal jurifprudence, which in its endeavours
to reprefs, by example, the commiffion of crimes,
never lofes fight of its favourite object, the protection of innocence. To this object the forms
of practice, the rules of evidence, and all the
numerous precautions which enfure to the accufed a fair and impartial trial, feem principally
directed. But it is the imperfection of all human inftitutions that no advantage can be gain-
ed, but at the price of fome inconvenience;
and *that* fecurity of innocence, which is juftly
the boaft of this country, cannot be attained
without affording frequent opportunities for the
efcape of the guilty. The very means by which
it is effectually provided that no one fhall be declared guilty, unlefs his guilt be regularly proved,
muft, in the nature of things, often produce the
impunity of crime; and it follows from that
ftrictnefs of proceeding, which can on no account be difpenfed with, that an acquittal muft
as certainly attend a mere doubt of criminality,
and a mere defect of technical form, as the
fulleft exculpation from the charge.

5   An

An acquittal, therefore, is far from affording any abſolute preſumption of innocence, ſince it may, with perfect propriety, be produced by a great variety of other cauſes. That certainty of conſtruction reſpecting guilt and innocence which you ſeek to extend to an acquittal, can exiſt only in the caſe of a conviction. It cannot exiſt in both caſes; for if none be convicted, but ſuch as are indiſputably guilty, and none acquitted, but thoſe whoſe innocence has been incontrovertibly demonſtrated, what verdict is to be pronounced in thoſe caſes, (more numerous far than both the other deſcriptions united,) where either a doubt remains on the ſubject, or, without any ſuch doubt, ſome chaſin or informality impoſes on the tribunal the irkſome duty of pronouncing an unwilling abſolution?

The only certainty that a verdict of " Not Guilty" is meant to produce, or that, conſiſtently with the tenour of the judicial proceedings of this country, it can attain, conſiſts in its legal operation and effect. An acquittal affords a certainty to the party, that he is for ever ſafe from the pains and penalties of the law. The priſon, the pillory, and the halter, have no longer any terrors for him, unleſs by a freſh act he expoſe himſelf to a freſh danger. However, guilty,

guilty he may be in his own confcience, in the opinion of the Public, or even according to the evidence produced upon his trial, he has the fure protection of the Law, as much as the moft innocent, to defend him from the legal confequences of guilt. An acquittal is a bulwark, and God forbid that it fhould not be an impregnable one, againft all farther purfuit in refpect of the charge from which it abfolves. It affords a complete deliverance from that charge. But it is impoffible to collect, from the acquittal alone, whether it was produced by a manifeftation of innocence, or by a failure of that precifion which is indifpenfable to authorize a conviction, even fuppofing the Jury, whofe verdict it was, to have performed that duty to the Public which Juries often forget, when they indulge a falfe and miftaken lenity to the individual at the expence of the community. No one can judge, from the mere circumftance of an acquittal, whether the party accufed appeared upon his trial in a favourable or unfavourable light—whether he was able to remove all ground of fufpicion, or was proved to be deeply implicated in the crime laid to his charge —whether he came forth like gold tried by the fire, or obtained merely a hair-breadth efcape through a defect of form, a nice diftinction of law, or by the fophiftry of an Advocate. The evidence which might be infufficient to warrant a Jury to fay " Guilty," may induce the Public to fay, *take warning and fin no more*. Not a year paffes but numbers are acquitted, whofe trials convince both the Juries by whom they are, tried, and the World, of their guilt.

This, neverthelefs, is the utmoft perfection that the Conftitution has been able to obtain in the practice of its criminal jurifprudence: and, with all its difadvantages, it deferves admiration in its general refult, fince it produces the utmoft fecurity for innocence, although at the fame time it occafionally lets loofe dangerous and defperate offenders; who, emboldened by their efcape, and infolent in their impunity, return impenitent to their former courfes, and brave the tardinefs of that juftice which it is to be hoped will, fooner or later, confign them to the fate they fo richly deferve.

The new fyftem which you endeavour to introduce, would invert the whole order of judicial proceedings, and render trial by Jury a pernicious inftead of a falutary inftitution. It would impofe the *onus* on the accufed to eftablifh his

innocence,

innocence, rather than on the profecutor to fubftantiate his charge. It would render fufpicion tantamount to proof, and facrifice that fcrupulous adherence to rules and forms, which conftitutes the grand beauty of an Englifh Tribunal, and the chief fafeguard of an Englifh fubject. If an acquittal were decifive of innocence, it could take place only where innocence could be incontrovertibly demonftrated; and a conviction, inftead of requiring full proof of guilt, might be pronounced in a doubtful cafe; or *becaufe* the accufed could not free himfelf entirely from all imputation.

In fupport of fo harfh, odious and unjuft a fyftem, you pervert the well known and facred principle of Englifh Law, that *every one is prefumed to be innocent till proved to be guilty.* But is it poffible not to fee that the term innocent here means nothing more than *innocent in the eye of the law.*—that it is merely oppofed to that full demonftration of guilt which is required to juftify a conviction—and that the fole import of the maxim is, that no one can be expofed to the *legal* confequences of a crime, without a *judicial* declaration of his criminality? Is it poffible not to perceive that this benevolent adage is not only expreffive of, but that it flows neceffarily from, that extreme caution, with which the Law fecures

every

every one from punishment, until his guilt has been duly and regularly established: presuming him, till then, to be *legally* innocent, however guilty he may, in reality, be? A grosser instance of sophistry was never displayed than in this attempt to construe the term innocence to signify absolute moral innocence of the crime in question. To support such a construction, you must suppose guilt to attach not upon the crime but the conviction; that whatever the circumstances of the case may be, a man is free from all stain whatever, and pure as the new born babe, in respect of the charge, until he be found guilty by his Peers—And that the word " Guilty," pronounced by the Foreman of the Jury, has not only the marvellous effect of producing the criminality which it declares, and of involving the unhappy prisoner at once in all the depths of moral as well as of legal turpitude, but also a retrospective operation, back to the moment when the fact charged as criminal was done. Were it not an insult on the understanding to expose such wretched sophistry, it might be asked, whether if you were to see a murder committed, with every possible circumstance of aggravation, you would, in spite of the evidence of your own senses, presume the murderer to be innocent, because he might happen to be acquitted. Or, supposing that upon a charge of High Treason, (which the law requires

quires to be fupported by two witneffes in order to juftify a conviction) only one witnefs were to appear, would not the Jury be bound to acquit, although they were fully convinced, by the evidence of that witnefs, of the guilt of the prifoner? What becomes, then, of your doctrine, that an acquittal is conclufive of innocence?

Whatever opinion may be formed of the propriety of the late acquittals, it is perfectly clear, that upon the principle, that an acquittal implies entire innocence, the parties accufed would have met with a very different fate. The Counfel who addreffed the Juries on the part of the Prifoners, were much too prudent to argue upon that principle. They laboured the cafe upon very different grounds; and inftead of admitting that the Juries could acquit only in cafe they were fully fatisfied of the innocence of the accufed, their reafonings were founded upon the very converfe of that propofition. They tortured their ingenuity to convince the Juries that nothing could juftify a conviction but the fulleft proof of the charge up to its greateft extent,—*the actual con-fpiring againft the life of the* KING, in the literal fenfe of the term—that whatever degree of folly, rafhnefs, or even of criminality might attach upon their clients (whofe conduct they

admitted

admitted to have been reprehenfible), nothing fhort of fuch an intent, evidenced by clear and unequivocal proof, could warrant a Verdict of Guilty. It is true, one of thofe Counfel has, in the Houfe of Commons, abandoned thefe grounds; and, fecure of the acquittals which he had obtained by the very aid of fuch reafoning, he has endeavoured, like you, to deduce from them the *abfolute* innocence of his late Clients. But in fo doing, he was grofsly imprudent, for he thereby embarraffed, by anticipation, his future defence of the HARDYS, TOOKES and THELWALLS, by whom he may hereafter be employed. On fuch occafions he will, when reminded of his Parliamentary opinions, be reduced to the neceffity of facrificing either his confiftency or his Clients.

The doctrine that an acquittal is conclufive *of the innocence of the party*, being fo abfurd and unconftitutional, what fhall be faid of their reafoning, who argue from an acquittal to the *non-exiftence of the crime?* If the accufed, although properly acquitted, may be undoubtedly guilty; who but an accomplice, dreading a farther inveftigation, or, at leaft, a favourer, from fome collateral motive, of the criminal project, would attempt from thence to infer that the offence had not been committed? Such, however, is the

2   abfurdity

abfurdity with which you are chargeable, when
in fupport of your *affected* difbelief of the exiftence of the Treafonable Confpiracy, you urge
nothing but the acquittal of the individuals accufed: But fo far were the Verdicts in queftion
from fpeaking the language you afcribe to them,
that, when viewed in connection with the whole
of the Trials, they carry with them the moft
fatisfactory proof that the Juries were fully convinced of the fact of the Confpiracy. It is alfo
certain, that thofe Juries confidered the conduct
of the Prifoners as highly criminal, and as extremely dangerous to the State, although from
fome *technical doubts*, that had been artfully in-
fufed into their minds, they might not think
themfelves authorized to declare the parties
Guilty of compaffing the death of the King.
Thofe doubts were not likely to be counteracted
by the indecent behaviour of the numerous
abettors of Confpiracy, who thronged the Tribunal during the whole of the Trials, and who
manifefted a lively and decided intereft in the
caufe and the fate of the Prifoners; and ftill lefs
by the hordes of banditti, who, (particularly during the laft Trial,) furrounded the Court, and,
in order to intimidate the Juries from convict-
ing, made its avenues refound with the moft
horrid menaces of riot and carnage; menaces
which derived an additional effect from the ex-

traordinary

traordinary conduct of the Chief Magiftrate of the City, who gave public notice that to pre-ferve the public tranquillity, he would not refort to Military aid. Such circumftances, though collateral, form a moft material part of the hif-tory of the Trials. Never before was Juftice fo flagrantly outraged in this Country. An influ-ence of the worft kind was exerted—the influ-ence of terror. Not to infift on the fecret threats that were diftributed (one of which is known to have been conveyed by letter to the houfe of a Juryman), the open appearances of a difpofition to tumult, in the event of a convic-tion, excited a confternation in the metropolis, and induced many perfons to dread the confe-quences of a Verdict which they confidered as due to Juftice. All the parties to the Confpiracy, all the affociates and co-adjutors of the Prifoners, openly efpoufed their caufe; and fucceeded in engaging the interference of the rabble, who were eafily perfuaded to think it *their* caufe. What precife effect fuch appearances really had upon the refult of the Trials, it may perhaps be diffi-cult to afcertain*; but certain it is, the fymp-toms

---

* If it be permitted to indulge conjecture refpecting the caufes that operated in producing acquittals, which were fo contrary to the prevailing expectation, the moft obvious gene-ral fuppofition, arifing upon the face of the proceedings *in Court,*

toms were fo alarming, that it was impoffible for the Jurymen to diveft their minds of the idea, that to convict might be fatal to themfelves and their families. Are thefe the means to which innocence reforts in order to repel an unfounded charge? Are thefe the proofs which convinced your mind that there was no Confpiracy?

Upon the whole, with regard to the only queftion of any future importance, the exiftence of the Confpiracy, all the circumftances at all connected with the fubject difplay that harmony and coincidence which are equivalent to *abfolute demonftration*. The uniform hiftory of domeftic

Court, and perhaps not the leaft reputable to the Juries, feems to be—that the firft acquittal was the effect of lenity and indulgence, the Jury confidering the humble and obfcure individual before them as a mere tool and inftrument of more able and dangerous men, fome of whom, they doubted not, would be convicted, and thereby the juftice of the Country would, as they thought, be fatisfied, and the benefit of example fufficiently enfured: that the fecond acquittal was pronounced becaufe, in point of fact, and perhaps through the influence of fuperior ability and forefight, lefs evidence was attainable in that cafe than in the firft: and the third, (which related to a cafe abundantly the moft grofs and flagrant of the three,) merely becaufe it had been preceded by two acquittals—a circumftance which, it is due to the Jury to obferve, *was moft unaccountably, and to the aftonifhment of every one, allowed fome weight in the conclufion of the Judge's charge.* This is an accurate, though compendious hiftory of the three Trials.

tranfactions for more than two years—the uninterrupted concurrence of facts, notorious to
all, and not difputed by any—the invariable impreffion made by thofe facts upon the public
mind—the refult of the moft deliberate and impartial Parliamentary inquiries—the folemn and
repeated Acts of the Legiflature—the finding of
the Grand Jury—the formal and elaborate inveftigation of the matter during three public
Trials—and, finally, the Verdicts of the Petit
Juries, when viewed in their connection with
the whole of the proceedings, and with collateral
occurrences—all thefe circumftances are in the
moft perfect and harmonious confiftency with
each other, and concur with united and irrefiftible force in eftablifhing the general and awful
charge—that a Treafonable Confpiracy has been
formed, for the purpofe of fubverting the Monarchy, and of abolifhing for ever the ancient
and glorious Conftitution of this Country.

THE GHOST OF ALFRED.

June 5, 1795.

.

LETTER

To the Right Hon. CHARLES JAMES FOX.

SIR,

IT is now above a year fince the moft dangerous and defperate Confpiracy ever detected in this Country was made the fubject of a charge of High Treafon :—a Confpiracy not merely againft the perfon of the Sovereign, but the whole frame of the Government, and the entire Conftitution, in Church and State :—a Confpiracy againft the very exiftence of Social Order :—a Confpiracy, in fhort, formed upon the model of the French Revolution, and purfued in concert with perfons who had brought their own King to the Scaffold, and who had projected the deftruction of all Kings, and of all Legitimate Authority. Although this charge was, in the opinions of many, brought home, in a manner fufficiently fatisfactory, to fome of the perfons moft deeply involved in the guilt of fo horrid an attempt, yet, without any irregularity in the forms of proceedings; without the fmalleft doubt as to the facts alledged; without even any doubt as

to

to the application of the Law to the cale,
Juftice was baffled in her endeavours to reach the
offenders, and the worft of all poffible crimes was
crowned with impunity.

To fuppofe that the Law does not confider fuch
a crime as penal in the higheft degree, would be to
infult moft grofsly the Jurifprudence of the Country. Although, indeed, a crime of fuch enor-
mous magnitude, and leading to. fuch fatal and
irreparable confequences, has never, in its full extent, been in the contemplation of the Legiflature (for what Legiflator could conceive, *à priori*,
a fyftem of fuch complicated mifchief and ruin,
as that which has affumed the title of the
" Rights of Man ?") Although this crime, is,
therefore, not to be found *precifely defined* in
the Statute Book, it comes, in the cleareft manner, within the fpirit of the provifions of the
Law againft High Treafon.—For while the grand
object of that Law feems to be the prefervation
of the King's Perfon and Authority, its real fcope
and effence are to fecure the Kingly Government,
in all its branches.

It is on account of the political character with
which the King is invefted, that all Treafons are
made referable to himfelf. All crimes, indeed, are
punifhable

punishable as offences against him, as being the Fountain of Justice: but High Treason is considered as more immediately pointed against himself, because it tends to the subversion of the Political State of the Country, of which he is " *Caput, principium, et finis.*" For such is his relative situation, that no harm can befal him without essential injury to the State; and, on the other hand, all attempts against the State tend, necessarily, to endanger his personal security.—While, therefore, for these reasons, his person is considered by Law to be so sacred, that to *compass* or *imagine* his death, is abundantly more penal than to perpetrate the murder of another individual; in point of legal guilt, the case is the same, whether the traitorous attempt be aimed against his life, or his political existence. In either case, the danger to himself is substantially the same; and the public danger is much greater in the latter instance, which is, therefore, in reality, the most aggravated, malignant, and destructive species of Treason. Upon this principle, a Conspiracy to depose him, or any step taken in pursuance of such a design, is invariably considered, in Law, as conclusive evidence of conspiring his death. For, I repeat it, the grand design of the Law of Treason, is not so much the preservation of the King in his natural capacity (though that, as essential to its main object, is provided for

with

, with the moſt anxious and affectionate ſolicitude), but in his Kingly Office, in his Regal Dignity, and in his Sovereign Authority; which Office, Dignity, and Authority, far from being confined to the immediate exerciſe of the Prerogatives of the Crown, extend, in the eye of the Law, to all the functions of Government, in the utmoſt latitude of the term. For, according both to the letter of the Law, and the genuine ſpirit of the Conſtitution, all Power, Dignity, and Political Excellence, centre in the King. He is the Sun of the Syſtem, communicating light, life, motion, and energy, to every part, and maintaining the whole in order, harmony, and coheſion. Through him are derived protection and ſecurity. So high and tranſcendent does the Law conſider him in his Royal character, that it aſcribes qualities to him in that character, which, as a mere man, it would be abſurd to ſuppoſe it poſſible for him to poſſeſs, but which it is highly beneficial to the Community * to conſider him endowed with as a King.

Thus,

---

* " The maſs of mankind will be apt to grow inſolent and refractory, if taught to conſider their Prince as a man of no greater perfection than themſelves." 1 BL. C. 242. If a ſentiment of reſpect to the Prince be of ſuch importance on general principles, how ſtrenuouſly ſhould it be maintained and inculcated at a time like the preſent, when ſuch indefatigable pains are taken, and ſuch artful means employed,

Thus, while the individual Members of the Dynasty submit, in their turn, like other persons, to the stroke of death, the KING is immortal[*]. So also, in that character, he is possessed of absolute perfection, and deemed incapable of doing any wrong[†]; nay, it is a crime not only to impute wrong to him, but even to canvas with freedom his *personal* acts, except in Parliament ; where, however, in order to preserve inviolate the respect due to his sacred person, without sacrificing thereto the necessary freedom of debate, those acts are always spoken of as the acts of the Minister[‡] : a fiction which has been too often perverted to the purposes of factious sedition, and made a cover for the violation of the very principles it was intended to preserve[||]. The King of England is also legally and exclusively invested with the attribute of Sovereignty, which he

derives

ployed, to loosen and dissolve the bands of Society, by exciting a contempt for all Legitimate Authority, and by persuading the People that they are under no obligations of duty or allegiance—that Government itself is an usurpation—and that the Sovereignty belongs to themselves.

[*] 1 BL. COM. 249.

[†] Ibid 245.

[‡] " But the privilege of canvassing thus freely the personal acts of the Sovereign, either directly, or even through the medium of his Ministers, belongs to no individual, but is confined to those august Assemblies." Ibid. p. 246.

[||] Thus Mr. GREY, in speaking of a Proclamation of the King, has been reported to say, that " A Proclamation had

been

derives from the only legitimate fource of authority, the Supreme Governor of the world, to whom alone (of courfe) he is accountable. " *Rex eſt Vicarius et Miniſter Dei in terrâ: omnis quidem ſub eo eſt et ipſe ſub nullo niſi tantum ſub Deo*.*" Every individual in the kingdom, of whatever rank or ſtation, is his Subject, and owes him allegiance. All Power is fubordinate to him, excepting only the Law; for he reigns only by Law, and that he does ſo is the moſt brilliant and valuable jewel in his Crown †. It is ſtated by the great authority laſt quoted, that, in " the exertion of lawful Prerogative, the King is, and ought to be, abſolute; that is, ſo far abſolute, that there is no legal authority that can either delay or

---

been iſſued on which he hardly knew how to expreſs himſelf, becauſe he could hardly diſtinguiſh whether the ſentiment that gave it birth was *more impotent or more malicious.*" Mr. Fox has been known to ſpeak with even leſs qualification or reſerve. " I ſtate it therefore to be my firm opinion, that there is not one fact aſſerted in *His Majeſty's Speech* which is not *falſe*—not one aſſertion or inſinuation which is not unfounded." And, afterwards, " the *Speech* goes on in the fame ſtrain of *calumny* and *falſehood*," &c. See DEBRETT's Parl. Rep.—Surely it would have been to conſult the dignity of Parliament, as well as the reſpect conſtitutionally due to the King, to have ſent forthwith to the Tower the utterers of ſuch ſhocking and diſloyal indecencies.

* BRACTON, lib. 1. c. 8.
† " Nihil enim aliud poteſt Rex, niſi id ſolum quod de Jure poteſt." Ibid. lib. 3. c. 9.

refiſt

refift him *." So likewife in his Legiflative capacity, that is, in enacting Laws, by and with the
advice and confent of the three Eftates of the
Realm, the Lords Spiritual, the Lords Temporal,
and the Commons, the King is Supreme. For
though, happily for the Liberties of this Country,
no Legiflative Act can pafs without the concurrence and participation of the two Houfes, which
form the Council of the King†, in the High
Court of Parliament, and which are therefore
properly termed "his Parliament :" yet the enacting
power is in the Crown—it is the King who is the ef-
ficient though not the fole Legiflator : and it is his

* 1 Bl. C. p. 250.

† " The King of England is armed with divers Councils,
one whereof is called *Commune Concilium :* and that is the
Court of Parliament—and another is called *Magnum Concilium :* this is fometimes applied to the Upper Houfe of Parliament, and fometimes out of Parliament to the Peers of
the Realme, Lords of Parliament, who are called *Magnum
Concilium Regis* ; for the proof whereof take one record for
many in the fifth yeare of KING HEN. IV. at what time there
was an exchange made betweene the King and the Earle of
NORTHUMBERLAND, whereby the King promifeth to deliver
to the Earle lands to the value," &c. " *per advice et affent
des Eftats de fon Realme et de fon Parliament eu autrement per advice de fen Graund Councell.* Thirdly, as every man knoweth,
the King hath a Privy Councell for matters of State. The
fourth Councell of the King are his Judges of the Law for
law matters." Co. LITT, 110. a.

" Habet Rex curiam fuam in concilio fuo in Parliamentis
fuis." FLETA, lib. 2. c. 2.

G   Will—.

Will—his *Fiat*—which gives to every Bill the force of a Law : as appears from the form and language, as well as of the Act itself*, as of the King's Assent to every public Bill which *he* thinks proper to be passed into a Law†. Nay, it is a part of his Royal Prerogative to convene, prorogue, and

---

* " Be it enacted, *by the King's Most Excellent Majesty*, by and with the advice and consent of the Lords Spiritual and Temporal and Commons, in the present Parliament assembled, and by the authority of the same ;" which enacting part of a Bill is in Money Bills introduced by the following most respectful and loyal terms: " Most gracious Sovereign, we your Majesty's most dutiful and loyal Subjects, the Commons of Great Britain in Parliament assembled, do most humbly beseech your Majesty that it may be enacted," &c. The forms of Parliament are the most faithful, authentic, and durable, as well as ancient records, both of the rights and of the duties of Parliament ; and it would be well if those persons, who wish to form just and accurate notions upon this important subject, would draw their information from such sources, and from the writings of respectable and long established Law Authorities, who, to deep study, have superadded the correcting and maturing influence of observation, reflection, and experience, rather than from the works of theorists and visionaries, whose views of things (notwithstanding their disposition to flight and romance) are as contracted as the closets where they pass their lives—from those of Party Writers, who represent every thing according to their own prejudices, or as it suits their purposes—or from those of presumptuous Foreigners, who fancy themselves qualified to instruct Englishmen in the History and Principles of their Laws, and in the Constitution of their Government.

† " Le Roy le veut."

diffolve thofe auguft Affemblies; and it is by virtue of that Prerogative, that the Members of each occupy their high and important ftations: the Lords being all, either in their own perfons, or in thofe of their anceftors, created by him, and the Commons being all fummoned by his writs.

Such are the important and dignified fituation, ftate, and character of a King of England, and in refpect of which the Law has fo anxioufly provided for his fafety. The avowed and apparent object of that Law is the fecurity of the King; becaufe, as it was admirably expreffed by a Learned Judge, " in fecuring the Perfon and Authority of the King from all danger, the Monarchy, the Religion, and the Laws of our Country, are incidentally fecured. The Conftitution of our Government being fo framed, that the Imperial Crown of the Realm is the common centre of the whole; and all traitorous attempts upon any part of it, are inftantly communicated to that centre, and felt there*." But the Law would

---

* See the Charge of the Lord Chief Juftice Eyre, to that moft refpectable and independent Grand Jury, who prefented, upon their oaths, that Thomas Hardy, John Horne Tooke, John Auguftus Bonney, Stewart Kyd, Jeremiah Joyce, Thomas Wardle, Thomas Holcroft, John Richter, Matthew Moore, John Thelwall, Richard Hodgfon, and

John

would be ſtrangely inconſiſtent with itſelf, if it did not guard, with equal care and anxiety, that ſituation, ſtate, and character, on account of which it ſets ſo high a value on the life of him to whom they belong. What abſurdity would it be, if an endeavour to overthrow the whole Government, if an attack upon the Conſtitution in the aggregate, were not conſidered as equally penal, and puniſhable with as much ſeverity as

John Baxter, as falſe Traitors againſt our Lord the King, their ſupreme, true, lawful, and undoubted Lord, did conſpire, compaſs, imagine, and intend to ſtir up, move and excite inſurrection, rebellion and war, againſt our ſaid Lord the King, within this kingdom of Great Britain, and to depoſe our ſaid Lord the King, &c. and to bring and put our ſaid Lord the King to death." And that, " to fulfil, perfect and bring to effect their moſt evil and wicked treaſon, and treaſonable compaſſings and imaginations aforeſaid, they the ſaid Thomas Hardy, &c. as ſuch falſe traitors as aforeſaid, did meet, conſpire, conſult, and agree among themſelves, and together with divers other falſe traitors, to cauſe and procure a CONVENTION and meeting of divers ſubjects of our ſaid Lord the King, to be aſſembled and held within this kingdom, with intent and in order that the perſons to be aſſembled at ſuch CONVENTION and meeting, ſhould and might wickedly and traitorouſly, without and in defiance of the authority, and againſt the will of the Parliament of this kingdom, ſubvert and alter, and cauſe to be ſubverted and altered, the Legiſlature, Rule and Government, now duly and happily eſtabliſhed in this kingdom; and depoſe, or cauſe to be depoſed, our ſaid Lord the King, from the royal ſtate, title, power, and government thereof, &c. &c."

an

an attempt to deprive the King of his Life! This
would be to make a part more valuable than the
whole, and the means more important than the
end. Yet to such forced and abfurd conftruction
of the Law, the Prifoners lately tried at the Old
Bailey, were chiefly indebted for their efcape.
For no perfon in the Country entertained a doubt,
that the object of thefe Culprits had been to fubvert the *whole* Monarchy. No perfon entertained
a doubt, that if their defigns had fucceeded, fuch
a fubverfion would have been accomplifhed. The
proof of this, arifing from the evidence adduced
on that occafion, and particularly from the written evidence which contained their own records
of their own proceedings, amounted to mathematical demonftration. But, becaufe it was not
proved that they meditated an immediate attack
upon the King's Life, the Juries were prevailed upon
to lofe fight of the King's Crown and Dignity—of his
Parliament—and of his Kingdom;—for the fake of
all which, an attempt againft his Life is declared
to be High Treafon. This could not have hap-
pened, unlefs thofe Juries, inftead of looking to
the Bench for that legal information, which they
could not conftitutionally derive, or honeftly
receive from any other fource, had fuffered themfelves to be mifled by the infidious reafonings of
Counfel, who, finding the facts unanfwerable,
had no other chance of faving their Clients than by

G 3   raifing

raifing doubts upon the queftion of Law; and who, in purfuance of this defign, inftead of fub- mitting, as they were in decency and in duty bound to do, their obfervations upon the legal part of the cafe, to the only competent and im- partial teft—the opinion and decifion of the Court, ' fought by legal conceits and perverfions, to bewilder the minds of the Jury in an inextricable labyrinth of fophiftry and chicane *.

In

* It is much to be lamented that Judges do not more frequently difplay that firmnefs, which is an in- difpenfable quality on the Bench, by interpofing their authority, in order to keep certain Practitioners at the Bar within the bounds of regularity and decorum; and, particularly, when thefe Gentlemen endeavour to ufurp the functions of the Bench, by pretending to lay down the Law to Juries. By repreffing fuch attempts, Judges would not only confult their own dignity, but the dignity of Juftice, the honour of its Tribunals, the purity of Judicial Proceedings, and even the refpectability of the Bar. The learned Gentleman who conducted the Defence of the State Criminals at the Old Bailey, was, at the Trial of the Dean of St. Asaph, on the point of being committed, by a Judge eminently diftinguifhed for all the qualities and endowments which can adorn that high ftation. If fuch commitment, which would have been fully warranted by the occafion, had taken place, it might perhaps have checked the Gentleman in *that* fyftem of invalidating the legal authority of the Bench, which he has fince purfued with too much fuccefs. What but error and injuftice could be expected to prevail,

if

In fuch manner, and for fuch purpofes, did they contend, in contradiction to the higheft legal

if Jures were to take their information on points of Law, from men who are hired to be partial, and who, however wrong, " are bound" (as was once expreffed by a Noble and Illuftrious Judge) " not to be convinced?" But it is principally in cafes of Sedition and Treafon, that the ftrenuous interpofition of the Bench is neceffary to keep thefe Gentlemen within their province: For it is in fuch cafes that they difplay their greateft zeal, and feem to exert, *con amore*, all their powers of fophiftry, in order to obfcure and pervert the Law, and " to make the worfe appear the better reafon :" and in thefe endeavours they meet with fuch fuccefs, that " it is eafier for a camel to pafs through the eye of a needle," than to bring an offender of that defcription to condign punifhment, although the times, beyond all former example, teem with treafonable and feditious practices. There is caufe for juft alarm, when fo many members of a profeffion, which fhould be moft confpicuous in the defence of Law, Order, and Government, feem not only difpofed, but eager, to encourage that fpirit of licentioufnefs and infubordination, which threatens the very exiftence of civilized Society. Thefe hopeful youths, who are trained up for " the feditious line," and who depend for their advancement, not on the *viginti annorum lucubrationes*, but on the triumphs of Sedition, will be much better qualified to make Frenchified Citizens than good Lawyers. It was not thus that a COKE or a HALE was formed. An honeft and confcientious Lawyer will confider himfelf as engaged in the fervice of his Prince, and he will think it his duty not to pervert, but to maintain the Laws. But the Advocate who proftitutes his tongue to the fervice of Faction, is the moft bafe and deteftable of characters. It was finely faid by

Lord

legal authorities, both ancient and modern, and to the uniform tenor of legal decifions upon the fubject, that nothing but pofitive evidence of a traitorous intention againſt the *natural* life of the King, could eſtabliſh the charge of compaſſing his death. If this doctrine were law, it would neceſſarily follow, that a Conſpiracy to depofe the King, would not amount to High Treafon. For, as the Statute makes no expreſs mention of fuch a Conſpiracy, unlefs it come within the deſcription of compaſſing and imagining the King's death, it cannot be brought within the 25th ED-WARD III. But the good fenſe of our anceſtors diſcerned clearly, that to deprive the King of his Crown would be to endanger his life, if not to enfure his deſtruction; knowing, that a depofed

Lord CLARENDON, that " every good Lawyer muſt of neceſſity be a Prerogative-man;" that is, he muſt be particularly zealous to fupport legal Prerogative. The fenſe and fpirit of the People will always be fufficient to prefeve their Rights, and to render an invaſion of them a chimerical attempt. But the Prerogatives of the Crown, which are of the very effence of the Conſtitution, and, *in effect*, among the moſt valuable privileges of the Subject, require every poſſible fecurity againſt the machinations of Faction, and the underminning encroachments of Popular Influence. The upright and diſcerning Lawyer will, therefore, be ever ready to ſtand forth in defence of thoſe Prerogatives, knowing, that by thus guarding the bulwarks of Order, he affords the beſt protection to rational and falutary Freedom.

Monarch

Monarch muſt be impriſoned for the ſecurity of
the Rebels; and that, for the ſame reaſon, " between the priſons and the graves of Princes, the
diſtance is very ſmall." Therefore, proof of ſuch
a Conſpiracy, though not accompanied with any
evidence of an intention to put the King to
death—nay, though accompanied with poſitive
proof (as far as ſuch proof would be attainable) of
an intention to ſave his natural life, and to pre-
ſerve him from all *bodily* harm, is, beyond all
doubt, concluſive evidence of compaſſing and
imagining his death. This conſtruction is ſup-
ported by the higheſt authorities, even admitting
the ſecurity of the King's perſon to be the ſole
object of this branch of the Law. It is laid down
by Mr. Juſtice FOSTER, that " the care which
the Law has taken for the perſonal ſafety of the
King, is extended to every thing wilfully and
deliberately done, or attempted, whereby *his
life may be endangered* *." And Lord HALE,
upon the ſame ſubject, ſays, " Though the Conſpiracy be not immediately, and directly and
expreſsly, the death of the King, but of ſome-
thing that in all probability muſt induce it, and
the Overt Act is of ſuch a thing as muſt induce
it; this is an Overt Act to prove the compaſſing
of the King's death †."—Upon the ſame prin-

* Foſt. 195.　　† 1 Hale, P. C. 109.

2　　　　　　　　　　　　　　　　　　　ciple,

ciple, this Learned Judge fays afterwards exprefsly, that " A confpiring to depofe the King,
and manifefting the fame by fome Overt Act, is
an Overt Act to prove the compaffing of the death
of the King within this Act of 25th EDW. III. *"
Nor is this construction lefs conformable to reafon than to law. It is, indeed, an exemplary
inftance of the truth of the maxim, that " the
Law is the perfection of Reafon." For what can
be expected to become of the King's Perfon, when
ftripped of this rule and authority ? where would
be the fecurity for his life, when deprived of his
Crown ?—The uniform experience of mankind,
and the invariable tenor of all hiftory, in relation
to fuch fubjects, furnifh a melancholy anfwer
to thefe inquiries; and the recent example of
France affords a dreadful confirmation of that
anfwer, and proves that a depofition, brought
about according to the fyftem of modern
Treafon, is equally fatal to the Sovereign, and
abundantly more fo to the State, than one effected
by the more direct and artlefs means known to
former times.

If, therefore, the confpiring to depofe the
reigning Monarch, which might, poffibly, have
no other object than to place a King _de jure_, in-

* 1 Hale, P. C. 111.

ftead

ftead of one *de facto*, on the Throne, be unquef-
tionably a cafe of the fpecies of High Treafon,
defcribed by the words, *compaffing the King's
death*, a Confpiracy to fubvert the Monarchy altogether, and to deftroy the entire frame of the
Government, muft, *à fortiori*, come within the
fame defcription. For the depofition of the King
is evidently included in the fuccefs of fuch a Confpiracy, though it be but a part of the mifchief
that would be effected by it.

Would the King be more fafe from the all-de-
ftroying fury of democratic rage, inftigated, in-
flamed and guided by defperate, unprincipled
and afpiring Demagogues, than from the ambition of a fuccefsful Rival. As far as he is indi-
vidually concerned, the diftinction between a private affaffination and a public execution, aggravated by the infulting mockery of the forms of
Juftice, conftitutes the whole difference between
that confpiracy to depofe him, which the higheft
legal authorities have declared to be High Treafon, and that Confpiracy againft his Government
which is framed upon the principles of the pernicious fyftem entitled the " Rights of Man," except, indeed, that againft the latter danger he can
derive no fecurity from any of his ufual means of
protection. But with regard to the State, the
difference between the fuccefs of thefe two modes
cf

of conducting treafon is immenfe; a difference which involves in it the maffacre or exile of the Clergy and Nobles, and of all individuals diftinguifhed for wealth or public virtue—the deftruction of all fecurity for perfons and property —the total fubverfion of all order and legitimate authority---the ferocious violence of popular fury ---and the unqualified but fluctuating defpotifm of ufurping Tyrants :---in one word, the accumulated and unfpeakable evils of Anarchy, and its infeparable attendant, Oppreffion; attended with the moft violent and dreadful internal convulfions; leading, in the natural courfe of things, to foreign War or foreign fubjection, and unavoidably productive of the complete ruin of the national refources, and of the annihilation of the national profperity.

That the Confpiracy, inftead of being directly aimed at the life of the King, pointed to this extenfive, complicated, and irremediable mifchief, which, befides its other dreadful concomitants, would have brought inevitable deftruction on the Perfon of the Sovereign, was, in reality, the fubftance of the defence urged at the trials at the Old Bailey, and the validity of which was recognized by the acquittals. It is true that thefe dangerous and deftructive defigns were mafked under the fpecious pre-

text

text of Parliamentary Reform; but this was, in fact, a very great aggravation of the crime, by pursuing it in a manner so artful and insidious, as greatly to increase the difficulty of repelling the attack, and to induce, under the influence of delusion, great numbers of even well-disposed persons to join in a plan, of which they did not suspect the real tendency or the ultimate object. It is a principle of natural justice, that the degree of criminality, in any case, is enhanced by treachery and disguise. The English Law so far adopts this principle, as to make disguise itself,, in certain situations, a substantive crime, without any act being done. No one can doubt for a moment that Parliamentary Reform was merely a pretext in the mouths of men, who sought to introduce the system of *Universal Suffrage* (a system the most fatal to the existence of Parliament that could possibly be devised), and who were proved, by their own papers, to have disclaimed all intention of applying to Parliament, and even to have declared Parliament incompetent to carry into effect designs, which they were determined to accomplish by their own strength. But it deserves to be noticed, that, independently of the nature of their object, the *means* they employed constituted a complete instance of the crime of High Treason. For it was proved by the same evidence, beyond the possibility of contradiction,

that

that in order to effectuate their object, whatever it
might be, they endeavoured to assume into their
own hands the authority and power of Government: and there was also indisputable proof of
their providing arms to assist them in the prosecution of this design.

Now, according to HALE and BLACKSTONE,
such attemps come clearly within that description
of High Treason, which is termed *levying of
War against the King.* These Authors indeed
allude, in that respect, to the cases of " levying
War," to pull down *all* inclosures, *all* brothels,
to remove counsellors *, to deliver generally from
prisons †, to alter the established religion ‡, &c.
Such attempts are described by HALE, upon the
authority of adjudged cases, as a constructive
levying of War, which is not so much against
the King's *person*, as against his *government* §.
And BLACKSTONE represents such acts, on account of " the universality of the design," as
" rebellion against the State, an usurpation
" of the powers of Government, and an insolent
" invasion of the King's authority"‖. But what
are such attempts compared with an endeavour,
not only to usurp the functions of Parliament,
and to assume the whole supreme authority,

* 1 Hale, P. C. 133.   † Ibid.   ‡ Ibid.   § Ibid.
‖ 4 Bl. C. 84.

but

but even to do that which, as declared by the offenders themselves, Parliament is incompetent to perform. This surely was the grossest possible instance of an endeavour to usurp the authority of Government, when it was meant to exercise that authority upon Parliament itself, and not only to supersede its power, but to destroy its existence, or, by new modelling it after their own pleasure, to make it the instrument of their execrable designs. This indeed was to attack the King in the noblest and most vital part, in his supreme Legislative character—in his High Court of Parliament. This would have been to sacrifice him on the very ALTAR of the CONSTITUTION.

The acquittal of the persons against whom such charges were substantiated, is indeed a phenomenon in the history of the Country—a phenomenon which can only be accounted for (paradoxical as such an explanation may appear) by attributing it to the unparalleled enormity of the offence ; which, because it so greatly exceeded, not only the experience, but the conceptions of former times, both in degree of turpitude and extent of mischief, was artfully represented as being out of the reach of the ancient Laws. Other circumstances might indeed contribute to give effect to such representations. The prosecution

was

was embarraffed by numberlefs impediments, which either arofe out of the ordinary courfe of proceedings, or were peculiar to the occafion. Such were, the impoffibility of producing any other witneffes for the Crown (however ftrongly the neceffity of fuch production might be fuggefted during the courfe of the Trials), than thofe whofe names were delivered to the Prifoners ten clear days before the arraignment, while the Prifoners were under no fuch reftriction *; the great and fcandalous infufficiency of the Pannel, many perfons being returned who were not compellable to ferve as Jurymen, for want of what is called a qualification : the neglect of adopting adequate meafures to compel the attendance of fuch Jurymen as were qualified, many of whom naturally chofe rather to incur a trifling penalty, than to engage in a fervice of.

---

* It was a Statute of W. III. that firft introduced a regulation of this nature—a Statute of which Bifhop BURNET fays, that " the defign of it was to make men as fafe in all treafonable confpiracies and practices as poffible." The mifchievous effects produced by this ftatute, have correfponded exactly with the defcription given by the Right Reverend Prelate of its defign, and impofe a duty upon the Legiflature to repeal it without delay. Why a different mode of practice fhould prevail on Profecutions for High Treafon and for Murder, unlefs it be with a view to facilitate the efcape of offenders of the worft defcription, it is difficult to conjecture.

fuch

fuch fevere duty: the great extent of the Prifoners peremptory challenges; which, together with
the two laft preceding circumftances, deprived the
Crown Officers of the benefit of *their* challenges,
and even obliged them to admit fome Jurymen
whom they had actually challenged, while it
reftrained them from challenging others, who were
known to have difplayed a zeal in favour of the
principles *, which had led to the perpetration of
the crime they were to try, and who, confequent-
ly, muft be fuppofed to feel a partiality in favour
of the Prifoners, although they could not approve

---

* Confidering the very great extent to which thefe principles have been propagated ; the many Clubs and Affiliated
Societies, the Divifions and Subdivifions, by which their influence is fpread and kept up through every part of the body
politic ; and the aftonifhing zeal and activity which all, who
are once profelyted to this new faith, difplay on every occafion at all connected with their caufe—confidering thefe circumftances, it may be too much to hope that a Pannel returned in a cafe of High Treafon fhould be free from any
mixture of perfons of that defcription. But if proper meafures were taken to render the Freeholders Book perfect,
and by continued attention to keep it fo, none but perfons
qualified in point of property would be returned ; and then,
if the Court would make it a rule to compel, by *adequate*
penalties, the appearance of thofe who fhould be fummoned,
there would always be a fufficient attendance to enfure a full
Jury, even after the Crown had challenged fuch as might be
difqualified in point of principle, and the Prifoner had made
his peremptory challenges, to the *very great extent* allowed
by Law in cafes of High Treafon.

of

of their conduct in its full extent ;—all thefe circumftances, (together with others, which it is
needlefs here to recount) had undoubtedly their
effect in producing the acquittals.   But, after all,
it is impoffible to account for the lamentable
failure of Juftice, without afcribing it, as its
primary caufe, to the magnitude and atrocity of
the offence, which confifted, not in an attack on
the King's natural Life, but in an attempt to
fubvert his Throne, and to ftab him through the
fides of the Conftitution.

THE GHOST OF ALFRED.

April 9, 1796,

LETTER

LETTER IX.

To the Right Hon. CHARLES JAMES FOX.

SIR,

IT required no great degree of difcernment to forefee that the acquittal of the State Criminals at the Old Bailey, would induce the neceffity of providing new laws againft Sedition and Treafon : Laws, which fhould not only be too explicit to admit of the perverfion which had been fo fuccefsfully employed in defeating the old ones, but which fhould have the effect of nipping Treafon in the bud, inftead of fuffering it to arrive at a ftate of maturity. Some perfons, indeed, were difpofed to believe that the *all but convicted* Traitors could be won by lenity ; that they could be wrought upon by a fenfe of their *wonderful* efcape, and induced thereby to abandon their criminal projects, notwithftanding their frequent and peremptory declarations to the contrary ; and that the Conftitution might even derive frefh fecurity from the impunity of thofe who plotted its deftruction. Thefe extravagant and abfurd expectations, which difplayed a total ignorance of the determined perfeverance of the difciples of the

H 2

new

new Philofophy, have been compleatly difappointed. The men, of whom fuch charitable hopes were formed, foon returned to their Seditious " vomitings," and to " their wallowing in the mire" of Treafon. Infenfible of the indulgence by which they had efcaped the fate they moft richly deferved, they have been rendered thereby but the more daring and indefatigable, in the purfuit of their mifchievous defigns. The Prefs has become more licentious and inflammatory, the Schools of Sedition have been more numerous, the Lecturers more animated, and their Pupils have been more frequently convened, not merely in their inftitutional Affemblies, where they learn the firft principles of the fcience, but alfo in the field, in order to train them to habits of difcipline; to infpire them with a confcioufnefs of their ftrength by a fight of their numbers; to enlift all who are difpofed for mifchief, under the banners of Difloyalty; and, by enuring the public to fuch affemblages, to leffen that falutary dread, which all very numerous meetings, and particularly when fo compofed, are calculated to infpire.

The horrid attack on the perfon of His Majesty on the firft day of the prefent Seffion, in his paffage to and from Parliament, was the natural fruit of fuch proceedings. If that attack had been permitted by Providence to produce

duce its intended effect, the unutterable calamity which it would have brought on the Nation, could only have been afcribed to the
operation of thofe licentious doctrines and inflammatory difcourfes, which had feduced the
multitude from their duty and allegiance; which
had infpired them with contempt for whatever they
had been accuftomed to hold in reverence; and
prepared them for acts of outrage and atrocity,
at the very idea of which, without fuch incite-
ments, they would have fhuddered. The connection between fuch a caufe and fuch an effect is
too obvious to be denied by any but the moft
profligate. It is not neceffary, indeed, in proof
of fuch a connection, to fuppofe that the fpecific
Treafon which blackened that dreadful day, was
actually hatched in the Committees of the Corre-
fponding Society, or that the wretches who fought
the life of His Majesty, were immediately
employed for that purpofe by the Lecturer of
Beaufort Buildings, or the Orators of Chalk
Farm, or of Copenhagen-Houfe. It is not on
fuch modes of Treafon that thefe men chiefly rely
to accomplifh their defigns. That they would
rejoice at the fuccefs of any attempt againft the
life of Majefty, it is impoffible to doubt, but
they would not expofe their plans to the failure
of fuch an attempt, nor themfelves to the proof
of having inftigated it.—They would be fools if
they did. Theirs, though a more flow, is, in

refpect

refpect of themfelves, a fafer fyftem, and much more fure in refpect of its object. They know better than to place their dependence on the hand of a lurking Affaffin, or on the favage fury of an enraged Mob. The horror, confufion and difmay attending the fuccefs of fuch means might be furmounted.——A fucceffor might avenge the horrid deed—and the glorious fcheme of Liberty and Equality might, in the refult, lofe ground. Their hatred is not againft the perfon of the KING, but his Throne: not againft the Monarch, but the Monarchy. The crime of Regicide, in order to anfwer *their* purpofe, muft be preceded by indignity, infult, and dethronement—by the fentence of a pretended High Court of Juftice, or of a Revolutionary Tribunal.——The Scaffold is their Altar of Liberty, where alone Royal Blood fhould flow, in folemn expiation of the unpardonable offence of wearing a Crown, and whence they might, at the fame time, proclaim to the World, the fubverfion of the Throne, and the extinction of the Monarchy. Such are the fcenes in which they afpire to act a diftinguifhed part; they review with rapture and exultation, the atrocities of that nature which already ftain the page of Hiftory; and they pant for an opportunity of adding to the lift of Royal Martyrs. Impatient for the renewal of fuch atrocities, they are clamorous for

Peace

Peace with the Muderers of the Gallic Monarch *,
who,

* It deferves, and it cannot efcape obfervation, that thofe
Perfons who are moft clamorous for Peace, are alike diftin-
guifhable for their zeal in favour of the French Republic,
and for their attachment to the principles on which that Republic is founded. They find that the War, contrary to the
expectation of thofe who provoked it, has proved the Palla-
dium of the Conftitution ; and, while it lafts, they defpair of
feeing the glorious fyftem of " Liberty and Equality" eftablifhed in this Country. But they look forward to a Republican
Peace as to a Republican Triumph ;—they expect it to prove
the vernal feafon of the " Rights of Man," which will foon
be fucceeded by a rich harveft of Treafon, Infurrection, and
Revolt ;—and they doubt not, that it will give to Government
much more difficult and embarraffing occupations, than the di-
rection of a War, by exchanging an honourable and conferva-
tive conteft with a foreign enemy, for fcenes of domeftic
ftrife and convulfion. They dwell with exultation on the
idea of an harmonious, fraternal, and uninterrupted inter-
courfe with their Gallic Brethren, with whom, alas! they
now can only fympathize at a diftance ;—they rejoice at the
profpect of the advantages which muft flow from an open
communication with the fuccefsful and irrefiftible Republic :
—But when they think of the arrival of a Republican Am-
baffador from France, and of his triumphant entry at St.
James's, then it is that their tranfports are at the height,
and they fhout their _Io Pæans_ in the higheft ftrains of extatic
rapture. Left, however, the incredulous fhould doubt
whether feelings fo bafe and unworthy can refide in Englifh
bofoms, let one of the Fraternity fpeak for the reft—

" For myfelf, who have exulted in the fuccefs of the French,
and the difgrace of their infolent and odious Foes, with a
keennefs of tranfport not to be defcribed, I have been long

H 4   prepared

who, by commemorating, have recently repeated
their crime ; and who by refolving that the infulting commemoration fhall be annually repeated,
have fairly and candidly announced to all Crowned
Heads, their determination never to abandon their
regicidal principles.

prepared to hail the triumphant entry of a Republican Re-
prefentative; and fhall exclaim, with equal fincerity and
rapture,

> " Dicite Io Pœan, et Io bis dicite Pœan."
> " Oh ! may I live to hail that glorious day,
> " And fing loud Pœans through the crouded way."

In another paffage, the fame Author fpeaks of " the neigh-
bouring influence of the French Republic ; not her arms, but
the *filent and tranquil operation of her principles, on our character, our manners, and our policy ;—an imperceptible, efficacious energy ! which nothing can preclude, nothing can
counteract, and nothing eventually refift.*"—See " A Reply
to the Letter of EDMUND BURKE, Efq. by GILBERT WAKE-
FIELD, B. A."—Thanks to Mr. WAKEFIELD for fo apt an
illuftration of a Republican Peace.

———————

How ftrikingly has the experience of Genoa, Venice,
Switzerland and America, confirmed the prophetic fuggeftions contained in the foregoing note ! Surely no further
proof can now be wanting to convince mankind, that in order
to procure the bleffings of Peace, they muft unite for the overthrow of the French Republic. Peace with that Republic
has invariably proved, and will continue to prove a much
greater misfortune than War. *Editor's Note.*

But in order to bring about, in this Country, a ſtate of things which would lead to ſuch a criſis, theſe Conſpirators are fully aware that they muſt cautiouſly abſtain from intermediate violence, which, by exciting general diſguſt and alarm, would tend only to fruſtrate their projects. They have too much ſagacity, and too intimate a knowledge of the nature of man and of ſociety, not to diſcover that their beſt chance for ſucceſs is by corrupting the public opinion and principle. To effect this, they want nothing but an uninterrupted acceſs to the public mind. If they could, by an un-limited licence in ſpeech and writing, obtain per-miſſion to utter whatever ſentiments, to pro-mulgate whatever opinions, and to inculcate whatever principles they pleaſe, upon all ſub-jects relating in any reſpect to Government, they are morally certain of being able, by degrees, to poiſon the minds, to excite the diſcontent, and to inflame the paſſions, of the maſs of the People, to ſuch a degree, that it would become impoſſible to reſtrain the exerciſe of the "*ſacred right of inſur-rection.*" They, therefore, with great wiſdom and conſiſtency, avoid every thing that favours of com-motion; they cautiouſly refrain from preſent violence, becauſe it might interfere with their ſchemes of future and more complete violence.— They are perpetually boaſting of the open and peaceable manner in which their followers aſ-ſemble and diſperſe. They are conſtantly re-

peating

peating that the only weapons which they employ are reafon and argument ; and, with great earneft-nefs, and equal fincerity, they exhort their pu-pils to avoid every appearance of tumult and dif-order.✝ In fhort, they artfully profefs to confine all their pretenfions to the facred right of free difcuffion ; and they difclaim, in the moft fo-lemn manner, all recourfe to other means. This is all they appear to require, and, indeed, all they actually want, in order to enable them to effectuate their defigns. They well know, that this fair and fpecious privilege, harmlefs in appearance as it feems to be, nay, valuable and beneficial as it really is, when fubjected to wholefome regula-tions and reftraints, is capable of producing the

✝ The Lecturer, who makes a livelihood by the fale of his Seditious Poifon, fhortly before his labours were interrupted by the calls of juftice, fuffered himfelf (rather unguardedly, it is true), to avow his confidence in the means employed by him and his coadjutors. Wifhing to difcourage fome fymp-toms of impatience, which his audience had manifefted rather boifteroufly, on the delay of his appearance beyond the ap-pointed hour, he took the opportunity to caution them againft every appearance of tumult or commotion ; obferv-ing, that " the means they profeffed to employ, were not only more fafe and eafy, but alfo infinitely more efficacious than open force ; that, by continuing, in a quiet and peace-able manner, to exercife the ineftimable privilege of *free difcuffion*, they would do more to promote the attainment of the important objects they had in view, than by the aid of myriads of men in arms, or by the moft powerful artillery, *were they difpofed to refort to fuch means.*"

utmoft

utmoſt extremes of violence, confuſion, and anarchy: confequences ſo different from the mild and gentle character it aſſumes, that it requires more penetration, and a greater faculty of reaſoning from cauſe to effect, than mankind in general poſſeſs, to be able to foreſee them. But the active and expert Profeſſors of the New Philoſophy are better inſtructed;—they are fully aware, that difcuſſion, in the unlimited ſenſe in which they claim the right, and in the exceſs to which they mean to carry it, is a powerful engine for the ſubverſion of Government—a mighty Lever, ſufficient, if judiciouſly applied, to overturn the Social Order of the whole World.

But although the Seditious Clubs, and Affiliated Societies, with their active and indefatigable Leaders, may, for the reaſons above ſtated, be fairly acquitted of any direct interference, and indeed of any privity, in the flagitious attempt recently made againſt the moſt valuable Life in the Kingdom, they muſt, in the judgment of every thinking perſon, be convicted of having produced the danger to which that life has been expoſed. They were the primary and predifpoſing, though not the operative, cauſe, of the ſhocking outrage. They had excited the ſpirit of diſloyalty, which broke forth on the occaſion, and which, though it be neceſſary for their future purpoſe, it would have been their intereſt to reſtrain, reftrain, until the time had come when it might be let loofe with more certainty of effect. The Mine they had been long preparing, exploded before it was complete: but although it failed, for that reafon, to produce its intended effect, and although they were unprepared to take advantage of the fudden explofion, it is not the lefs true that the combuftibles were collected and arranged by themfelves.—Thus the defigns of the wicked are fometimes defeated by the very means employed for their accomplifhment.

It pleafed an over-ruling Providence to guard the facred perfon of His Majesty in the hour of danger, in gracious token, it is to be hoped, that he is deftined long to reign over a grateful and a loyal People, and at length to tranfmit the Crown of thefe Realms to an illuftrious race of defcendants, who will not only fway his fceptre, but inherit his virtues. There is even reafon to hope, that good will arife out of evil; and that the abortive attempt to perpetrate the worft of crimes will, in its confequences, be productive of additional fecurity to the Conftitution. The horror, alarm, and indignation univerfally excited on the fhocking occafion, inftantly fuggefted the indifpenfable neceffity, not only of making farther provifion for the fafety of His Majesty's Perfon and Government, but alfo of guarding, by wife and efficacious meafures, againft the cause,

which

which having, by a partial and premature operation, produced such effects, shewed, in the most
striking manner, to what consequences it would
lead, if not seasonably and effectually checked.—
With a view to such important objects, and in
compliance, as well with the earnest wishes of
the Nation, as with the imperious call of circumstances, two Laws have been made, which,
in conformity to the wise principle that had
presided over the formation and progress of the
British Constitution, were adapted to the exi-
gency of the case, and to the nature and extent
of the mischief they were intended to remedy.
The provisions of these Laws have been too
much discussed, and are too well known, to require any comment.—Suffice it to say, that their
great excellence consists in their being calculated
still more for prevention than cure, by tracing
Sedition to the seminaries where it is inculcated,
and by crushing Treason, while in embryo, instead of suffering it to acquire the form and con-
sistence of *Overt Acts.* In passing such Laws, on
such an emergency, the Legislature performed a
duty, the omission of which would have amounted
to the basest treachery—to an absolute surrender
of all those interests, which it was its bounden
duty and most important object to preserve. But
upon the passing of these Laws, a duty equally
solemn and indispensable devolved on the Executive Government. whose province it is to take

care

care that they do not remain a dead letter on the Statute Book. Should it be permitted either directly to infringe, or indirectly to evade them with impunity, the People will be apt to despise the authority by which they were made; and thus they will be even instrumental in accelerating the mischiefs they were intended to prevent. It therefore behoves the Crown Officers and the Magistracy to exert their utmost vigilance and activity in giving effect to these salutary Laws, and in convincing the ill-disposed, that as often as they offend, their conduct shall be subjected to legal investigation.* But

---

* Notwithstanding all the approbation to which the principle and the provisions of these Laws are entitled, it is impossible not to discover a deficiency of prudential spirit and firmness, as well in restricting their duration to the short period of three years, as in deferring, to a second conviction, the possibility of subjecting seditious practices to the penalty of transportation. It is surely to renounce all idea of proportion between crimes and punishments, to inflict death or transportation for many of those offences which are thus punished every day by the English Law, and to suffer the crime of Sedition, which leads, in its ordinary operation, to treason and revolt, and, in its modern tendency, to all the horrors and miseries of civil anarchy—which is the parent of all the crimes and of all the calamities that can afflict society— to suffer such a crime to pass through all the stages of guilt, which must, in all probability, precede a second conviction of the same offender, before it can meet with the only punishment applicable to an offence of that description. If in all the criminal codes by which justice is administered, or in all the systems created by fancy for its more perfect administration, there be one punishment more strikingly apposite to its

But all the wisdom of the Legislature, and all the energy of the Executive Government will be of no avail, unless Juries resolve to act with firmness in their important functions. Their situation, on such occasions, is undoubtedly arduous and embarrassing. During the Trial, they have to resist all the arts of persuasion—all the charms of eloquence—all the efforts of ingenuity, which are sure to be exerted, in order to excite in their minds a doubt of guilt; a doubt which as certainly produces an acquittal,

as

its correspondent offence than another, it is that of Transportation, when applied to the crime of Sedition. What can be more just or equitable, in respect of the offenders, than to send out of a Country those who not only dislike, but who endeavour to overturn, its political establishments, and who seek to inspire their fellow subjects with the same spirit of discontent, restlessness and disaffection, by which they are themselves actuated? What can be more judicious and salutary in respect of the state, than to expel those noxious humours, which not only generate disease, but, by their contagious quality, tend to corrupt the whole mass of juices in the body politic? Besides in respect of this class of offenders, there is no penalty, short of Transportation, that operates as a punishment. The Pillory is to them (as it has been called in appropriate language) " the stepping stone to glory." Fines imposed upon them are levied by the voluntary contributions of a numerous fraternity; and Prison is but the theatre of their triumph, where they brave the laws by the most daring and flagrant repetitions of their offence—where they are loaded with the caresses and the presents of the disaffected—where they hold assemblies of conspirators, to contrive fresh plots against the State—where they open new

schools

as a demonftration of innocence. Againft fuch artifices they fhould ever be on their guard, remembering that it is the duty of the Judge, not only to give them all the affiftance in his power, by developing complicated facts, and by communicating to them the law as it applies to thofe facts, but alfo to act as Counfel for the Prifoner, and to take care that he have the benefit of every fair advantage that arifes in his favour, either from the law or the fact.

It is not, however, in open Court that lioneft and confcientious Jurymen have the greateft difficulties to encounter. Their moft arduous tafk

fchools of Sedition, and find it an eafy matter to repel the effects of wholefome correction, and to infufe the poifon of difloyalty into minds already inured to habits of licentioufnefs—and whence, at length, they return to their homes with exultation, and with confirmed difpofitions and increafed powers for mifchief.

In allufion to the foregoing obfervations refpecting prifons, the Editor begs leave to call the attention of the Sheriff of London to the Police of Newgate, where Culprits confined for feditious practices have been even allowed to paint their rooms with the National colours of France, and to infcribe on their doors the words, "Citizen——*Palais Légalité.*" If, after all, it fhould be found neceffary to retain imprifonment as one of the punifhments for fedition, in its lighteft fhades, it fhould furely be adminiftered by way of *folitary confinement.* This would in reality be a falutary punifhment, and conduce to reformation. Even Mr. Erfkine, though incapable of fedition, would fhudder at the idea of being left to filence and reflection for fix months.　　　　　　*Editor's Note.*

is probably yet to come, when they have sur-
mounted all the efforts of sophistry, and all the
arts of false colouring, and when they are satis-
fied, after a diligent and impartial investigation,
that the charge is fully established, and that it
only remains for them to pronounce the awful Verdict of " Guilty"—If, upon retiring to consider of
their Verdict, they happen to find among them
one or two individuals infected with the *influenza*
of the *Rights of Man*, it is then that their situation is most difficult and painful. They then see
themselves reduced to the disagreeable alternative
of either sacrificing the obligation of their oaths,
or of engaging in an obstinate contest with men,
who are pre-determined not to convict; and who
are generally possessed, in an eminent degree,
of qualities which fit them for such a conflict. Considering the great extent of the ma-
lady above mentioned, and the indefatigable
industry with which those, who are under its influence, endeavour to worm themselves into every
situation where they can serve their favourite cause,
it is but too probable that such a mixture will be
found in a Jury impannelled to try a charge of
treasonable or seditious practices *. Sensible that

in

---

* To preserve the administration of Justice from so poi-
sonous a mixture, the suggestions contained in the last Letter
respecting the Freeholder's Book deserve consideration. To

I   those

in no other fituation they can render fuch effectual fervice to that caufe, they fail not, upon fuch occafions, to difplay the utmoft zeal, fervour, and perfeverance. No matter how ftrong the proofs—how aggravated the cafe—how large the majority for a conviction---all fuch confiderations they fet at defiance, and declare that they will rather perifh in the conteft, than confent to a Verdict of " Guilty."

The unanimity which the law requires, in the delivery of a verdict, affords, in fuch cafes, but too favourable an occafion for perverfenefs and obftinacy to prevail over candour, moderation, and juftice; and, unfortunately, the fpirit, refolution, and perfeverance of the well-difpofed are generally unequal to the ardour and pertinacity of thofe, who are under the guidance of paffion, or the influence of Party confiderations. There is but one fair and equitable

thofe fuggeftions it may be proper to add an admonition to worthy and well-difpofed Jurymen to make a point of attending the Court whenever they are fummoned upon a charge of Sedition or Treafon. The want of fuch attendance frequently occafions a deficiency of the Jurors returned upon the Pannel; which deficiency is generally fupplied by perfons of the fame principles and views as the Prifoner; who, neglecting no opportunity of promoting their grand object, always throng the Court on fuch occafions, and prefent themfelves eagerly to fill the office which honeft and fober men are too folicitous to avoid.

rule

rule for the attainment of unanimity in any body of men, poffeffing equally the right of individual fuffrage---namely, that the Minority fhould yield to the voice of the Majority. It is thus alone than even a fmaller number than twelve perfons can reafonably expect, even on ordinary occafions, to concur in will, or to act in concert; and unlefs this rule be applied to the deliberations of Juries, the neceffity of an unanimous concurrence in their determination, will not only fubject that mode of trial to the charge of extreme abfurdity, but alfo render it abfolutely incompatible with juftice. In criminal cafes, and particularly in capital ones, the feelings of a Jury will always be inclined fo far to qualify this rule, as to require fomething more than a mere turn of the fcale to produce a conviction, and a bare majority will ever be ready to furrender their opinion to the confcientious fcruples of thofe, who may incline to a more merciful verdict. It would, indeed, have ftamped a much greater degree of apparent perfection on the inftitution of Trial by Jury, if, inftead of a *nominal* unanimity being a requifite quality in a verdict, the principle had been exprefsly eftablifhed, that a majority, confifting of two-thirds, or three-fourths, fhould be fufficient for a conviction. But the good fenfe, moderation and humanity of the Englifh character have fupplied, in this cafe, the want of pofitive

I 2 regula-

regulation, by generally adopting, in practice, so rational a principle. Nor can a better proof be wanted, that a case is proper for conviction, than the willingness of eight or nine English Jurymen to convict.

But although the votaries for the new philosophy profess to maintain, as one of their fundamental doctrines, the right of majorities to decide on *all* questions whatever, (and even in those cases of social and political relations, where such a principle is incompatible with the existence of that sovereignty on the one hand, and of that subordination on the other, which are of the very essence of the connection), yet, when it suits their purpose, they are the first to violate this principle, by insisting that their own notions, projects and systems, shall prevail over the greatest superiority of numbers. They seem to think themselves exceptions to the rule which they lay down for the rest of the world; as if, by the aid of the new light, they were possessed of absolute infallibility, or, at least, of such superlative wisdom, as to entitle them to dictate to the whole human race, and to supersede every ancient establishment. Thus, when such persons find themselves (in however small a proportion) in a Jury, met to decide on an offence against the State, as such a case comes immediately within the compass of their

reforming

reforming or revolutionary zeal, they reckon as nothing the clear and decided opinion of nine or ten of their fellows, who think that the demands of juftice can only be fatisfied by a verdict of Guilty—and they expect the majority, however great, to conform to their pleafure, and to acquiefce in their determination to acquit. Nor is this perverfity confined to the active abettors of the diforganizing fyftem, or to thofe who feek for profit or perfonal confequence in a new order of things. When once the baneful contagion has feized the mind, the moft refpectable and opulent perfons act as if they were reduced to the moft defperate circumftances, or influenced by the bafeft defigns. They can never fee any guilt in confpiracies againft the Government. If a criminal, charged with fuch practices, has but taken care to borrow the cloak of Reform, or to affume fome other pretext of a fpecious and impofing nature, he is fure to find favour in their fight: nay, fo far does the influence of this fympathizing fpirit extend, that Sedition and Treafon, in every form, are become facred crimes, and muft not be punifhed, even though they quit the wily and circuitous paths, difcovered by modern practitioners, for the more direct and open road frequented by confpirators of ancient times. Of this a ftriking inftance has recently occurred, where (it is faid) the violence and obftinacy of two fectaries pre-

I 3   valled

vailed over the fenfe and fpirit of the reft of the
Jury, by forcing an acquittal in a clear cafe of
inartificial Treafon of the old ftyle, conducted
according to ancient forms, and deftitute of any
of the fubtleties and refinements of modern in-
vention *.

It

* In the cafe here alluded to, the Prifoner was proved,
beyond the poffibility of contradiction, to have correfponded
with the King's Enemies, and, in the courfe of that corre-
fpondence, to have given them, at their defire, the beft information his induftry and artifices could procure, of the internal ftate of the Country, in order to enable them to judge of
the expediency of attempting an invafion. It was not difputed that he gave them true information and faithful advice ; fuch information and advice as were calculated to preferve them, and which, in all probability, did preferve them
from an enterprize, in which they muft inevitably have ex-
perienced difappointment and defeat. In fhort, the charge
was fo fully and clearly eftablifhed, that it was out of the
power of ingenuity to devife any other defence than that he
was induced, by the refult of his enquiries refpecting the
ftate of the Country, and in faithful difcharge of the truft
he had undertaken, to diffuade them from their project of invafion—And although in fo doing he rendered them a moft
important fervice—although the very fame principle on
which he acted would have led him to invite the Enemy to
the Britifh fhores, if he could have held out to them a rational profpect of fuccefs, he was abfolved from the charge
of High Treafon by a verdict, produced by the influence
above defcribed!

As the names of perfons who fill a public character on
important occafions cannot be too generally known, it is

2   thought

It would, however, be impoffible for this pernicious influence to gain fuch an afcendancy in
the deliberations of Juries, were it not for the aid
or a fentiment of falfe humanity, which is moft
artfully excited, and which alone could reconcile
the majority of a Jury to the idea of acquitting
a man, of whofe *guilt* they were *convinced*.---
Thinking that their error may be excufable, if
they err on the fide of Mercy, they are thereby
induced, after a fhort refiftance, to furrender
their own opinion to the captious oppofition of
one or two individuals. But, in yielding to fuch
impreffions, they lofe fight of the nature of their
fituation; of the oath they have taken, to give *a*
true verdict according to the evidence; and of
the confequences which may enfue a departure
from their engagement. It is not *their* province
to exercife lenity and indulgence, but to admi-
nifter juftice.---Being fatisfied, on fair grounds, of
the guilt of the party, nothing can abfolve them
from the obligation of declaring that guilt; and

thought proper to fubjoin a Lift of the Jury who acquitted
Mr. Stone.

John Leader,	Thomas Burnett,
John Mayhew,	William Sumner,
John Hetherington,	John Lorkin,
Thomas Cole,	Peter Taylor,
Charles Minier,	William Weft,
Daniel Dyfon,	Ifaac Dimfdale.

if

if they fuffer themfelves to be prevailed on, by any confideration whatever, to pronounce a different verdict, they infringe their oaths, betray the folemn truft repofed in them, and violate the moft facred duties of morality and religion. The quality of Mercy is the prerogative of the Crown; and it is one of the numerous excellencies of the Monarchical Conftitution of this Country, that this amiable prerogative is fure to be exercifed, whenever its interpofition would not be productive of public mifchief. But when Juries fuffer themfelves to be influenced by fuch motives, they ufurp a function which does not belong to them; they facrifice the fundamental principles of that admirable inftitution, of which they form a part; and they render themfelves morally refponfible for the confequences. Befides, they moft grofsly deceive themfelves, when they imagine, that in acquitting the Guilty, they yield to the dictates of Humanity. It is a falfe, pernicious, and cruel humanity which they indulge. They are chargeable with the moft complicated, extenfive, and barbarous *Inhumanity*. In faving the Guilty, they punifh the Innocent. In a cafe of High Treafon, particularly, they decide between the Prifoner and the Country at large; and, for aught they know, the fate of each is equally in their hands. When, in fuch a cafe, they fpare a life which is forfeited to the Laws, they endanger the

lives

lives of millions—the fafety of their Sovereign—
the fecurity of the State—and the exiftence of
the Conftitution. The Acquittals at the Old
Bailey led, by a natural and obvious progreffion,
to the fhocking outrage that expofed the Kingdom
to the greateft of misfortunes, and that might have
been productive of calamities which would defy
the utmoft ftretch of imagination; and fcarcely was
the acquittal of STONE pronounced, when another
atrocity of the like nature furnifhed an additional
proof that the daring and licentious fpirit, which
had been excited among the lower orders, could
not be repreffed without the aid of example—
whereby the multitude fhould be convinced, upon
the evidence of their own fenfes, that they are
fubject to the Laws, and that crime cannot hope
for impunity.

It behoves Jurymen, therefore, to reflect very
ferioufly on the nature and importance of their
fituation, and to refolve on a firm and refolute
difcharge of their duty; fuffering themfelves neither to be feduced by the arts, intimidated by the
threats, nor vanquifhed by the pertinacity of
thofe who would prevail on them to return a Verdict which is not dictated by their confciences.—
Shall a large majority of refpectable and confcientious men, whofe only wifh it is to admini-
fter

ster impartial juſtice, become the mouth-piece of one or two fanatical Reformers, who can diſcover no guilt in any attempt againſt the eſtabliſhed Government? or, of a like number of determined Jacobins, who ſeek to accompliſh the deſtruction of all legitimate authority? In reſiſting the obſtinacy of ſuch characters, they muſt expect to undergo ſome perſonal inconvenience.—The conteſt may be arduous and the ſtruggle long. But it is a conteſt with Licentiouſneſs and Anarchy—it is a ſtruggle for Civil Liberty, Order, and the Conſtitution. They owe it to God and their conſciences—to their families and their Country—to the preſent age, and to poſterity, to perſevere.— If, however, they ſee at length no proſpect of being able to vanquiſh the inflexible ſtubbornneſs of the perverſe few, and there be found among the larger number ſome whoſe health will not admit of a farther conflict, (an inconvenience to which the majority are moſt expoſed), there is ſtill one method left by which they may diſcharge their conſciences, leſſen the evil they cannot entirely prevent, and convince the world that they have exerted themſelves to the utmoſt in the performance of a painful duty. Inſtead of returning an unexplained verdict, as in ſuch caſes they are apt to do, let them come into Court and ſtate the real fact—let them diſcloſe the conteſt teft in which they have been engaged, and point out the individuals who have obftructed the progrefs of Juftice. By fuch explanations they would deprive the Factious of that ground for boafting, and that occafion for triumph, which an unqualified acquittal ever affords them, and they would render the Patrons of Sedition lefs defirous of thrufting themfelves upon Juries, by convincing them, that although they may fucceed in fruftrating the claims of Juftice, they will be themfelves fubjected to that refponfibility of public opinion, which fhould ever attend the exercife of a public duty; while the acquittal itfelf, fo explained, would have, in a great degree, the effect of a conviction, by expofing the criminal to juft and general deteftation, which the impunity of his crime would ferve only to aggravate.

There cannot be a greater error than to fuppofe that Jurymen are not at full liberty to difclofe what paffes among themfelves.—Every one of them is perfectly free to make fuch difclofure, either openly in Court, or afterwards to the Public, in whatever manner his difcretion may fuggeft.—Petit Juries are not, like Grand Juries, fworn to fecrefy. If they retire, it is only that they may deliberate without interruption, and apart from all influence.—But they are not fubjected,

jected, either by the nature of their office, or the terms of their engagement, to any obligation of concealment. Grand Juries are bound by oath to " keep the King's council, their own, and their fellows:" because a difclofure of what occurs in that early ftage of the proceedings might defeat the ends of Juftice; but, as the decifion of the Petit Jury is fubfequent to the publication of all the evidence of the cafe, no poffible inconvenience can refult from the particulars of their delibera-tion being made known to all the world : nay, it is even a duty incumbent upon them, to expofe the improper conduct of any of their brethren, particularly if fuch conduct has had any influence upon the Verdict. In civil cafes, and alfo in cri-minal ones where a conviction has taken place, injuftice may, in confequence of fuch expofure, be remedied by a new trial : and, in all cafes, it would be productive of public advantage and ge-neral fecurity, were Jurymen to act under the impreffion, that, although for a time they are fecluded from the eye of the world, the circum-ftances of their behaviour, while in that ftate of retirement, will, if deferving of notice, be brought before the tribunal of the Public.

As an inducement to Juries to liften to thefe admonitions, let them remember that in çafes of

a fea feditious or treafonable nature, they are not merely the difpenfers of the law, but the guardians of the Conftitution. If the laws, which are made for the fecurity of Government, be rendered inefficient, for want of energy in thofe who are entrufted with their execution, the entire adminiftration of juftice—the exiftence of Trial by Jury itfelf—all the fafeguards of perfons and property—and all the rights and liberties of Englifhmen, muft give way to that diforganizing fyftem, which tends to the total fubverfion of civilized fociety. If Juries will not do their part towards carrying thofe laws into effect, they will render the inftitution of Trial by Jury a curfe inftead of a bleffing. The mifchief they will produce will infinitely more than counterbalance all the good they have ever done, or can ever do. They will crown with fuccefs the machinations of the Difaffected, and render the caufe of Anarchy triumphant.

The CONSTITUTION—that venerable fabric of Britifh glory and profperity—is guarded on all fides againft the encroachments of power; it is fecure againft the inroads of influence—it has nothing to fear from its open and avowed enemies, unlefs their attacks be favoured by the treachery or fupinenefs of thofe who are entrufted with its
defence.

defence. Should it ever perifh, its deftruction will be effected by the means provided for its prefervation.

THE GHOST OF ALFRED.

June 3, 1796.

FINIS.